ISBN-13: 9781735883236
ISBN-10: 1735883239

Cover illustration by: A L Watson
with additional design by: A S H
Printed in the United States of America

# BOOKS BY THE AUTHOR

*Where Dragons Die*

*A White Rabbit in Summer*

## Twisting the Turall

*Ether*

*Voyage*

*Gold*

# A WHITE RABBIT
# IN SUMMER

### ASH

*For the adults who still spend half their life in dreams.*
*For the children who had to grow up too fast.*
*For those who had to find their way on their own.*

*And by request, for Yvette Blalock.*
*I hope you gave up your quest for truth and*
*found a truly unconditional love.*

# INTRODUCTION

He'll see my body and regret what we weren't. Maybe it won't happen like that. Maybe he'll hear about my death from a friend or a teacher, but he'll know that I'm gone and realize what a mistake he made by never giving us a chance. I don't blame him. He's not like me. He can't see the rainbow of time like I can. He doesn't know how beautiful we are together.

All Jad can see is my shabby sweater and Fifi's glossy bubblegum smile. Maybe it's not even about her, maybe it's all about how his friends look at me. I know that Jad likes me. I've seen him smile for real. I've heard how he laughs with her and it's nothing like how he laughs when he's with me. He's laughing because he knows he needs to and not because he thinks she's half as clever as that bitter fudge cookie thinks she is.

I don't want to take my life, I just want him to know what it would be like if I left this world. I want him to know that he made a mistake. I know what you're thinking, Diary, but I promise you I've thought about this. Please don't talk to the Royals, Diary. I can do this myself!

I've been practicing my speech. I can get out my request without frowning or tearing up. When I start thinking about the questions they'll ask, that's when I start having trouble. I know that they're just trying to help me. I know they're on my side, but right now it feels like the Magicals are in my way. There's reason for them to worry. They love me, I know they do. I love them too, it's just that I've never loved anyone like how I love him. It's not enough to dream about him, I need to feel his hand with my own fingers. Living without him hurts too much.

I've spent a month talking myself into this. This isn't an impulse; it isn't! If I can go to the world without me, he'll realize how much he missed me, and he'll never look back. He'll hold me tight and only let go to eat. I want to see him eat. I want to see him smile at me again. Now he won't even look at me. Now he acts like we were always nothing. I can't live like this. I know I can't. Everyone who said that I'll get over it doesn't feel the blood sloshing around in my chest. They must not have ever been in love, because no one who's felt like I do could ever get over it!

I can't keep living like this.

I'm going to tell them.

I've been practicing my speech. I can get out my request without frowning or tearing up. When I start thinking about the questions they'll ask, that's when I start having trouble. I know that they're just trying to help me. I know they're on my side, but right now it feels like the Magicals are in my way. There's reason for them to worry. They love me, I know they do. I love them too, it's just that I've never loved anyone like how I love him. It's not enough to dream about him, I need to feel his hand with my own fingers. Living without him hurts too much.

I've spent a month talking myself into this. This isn't an impulse; it isn't! If I can go to the world without me, he'll realize how much he missed me, and he'll never look back. He'll hold me tight and only let go to eat. I want to see him eat. I want to see him smile at me again. Now he won't even look at me. Now he acts like we were always nothing. I can't live like this. I know I can't. Everyone who said that I'll get over it doesn't feel the blood sloshing around in my chest. They must not have ever been in love, because no one who's felt like I do could ever get over it!

I can't keep living like this.

I'm going to tell them.

# 1

**January 19**


I forced myself to go on a jog. It was supposed to make me happy, but it didn't. I ran all the way to the pond and I almost puked when I got there. I leaned against a tree and when the vomit didn't come, I cried. I held myself and cried. It wasn't the thought of leaving this world that made me cry, it was the thought that I hadn't done this earlier. I could've been with Jad all the way back in eighth grade when he bought me those kitty pencils. I talked myself out of it then, but this is different.

Oh, Diary, it's really going to happen! Jad is going to be my boyfriend! It feels so good to write that! I love him. I love Jad and nothing is going to keep us apart!

I just need to calm down. I took a shower and tried sitting and watching TV but my heart was pounding the whole time. I feel alive for the first time in months. I'm so happy I'm doing this. This is going to be the first day of my entire life, and it's going to be a life with Jad!

Princess Platypus is going to be the hardest to convince. I know she means well, but I'm not a kid anymore! I never abused my power! I took life as it came. I'm mature. I know how to handle the world on its own terms, it's just that this isn't the right world for me. Something went wrong along the way, I just need Captain Alligator to help her see that.

The Captain is always going on about how the timeline's been sheered by all the scrying and wanderers. This was never a power that I asked for. It wasn't a power that any of us asked for. And it's not like I want to use my powers to get famous or rich or something dangerous. I'm changing one event. Besides I'm going to a world where I'm not even alive so there won't be any time clones. The Cap will be on my side. He's always telling me to take a bite out of life, so I should, right?

Mama Koko worries me. I know that she'll be on my side, but she might not support my decision all the way. She always does that thing where she looks and smiles and says, "whatever you want," but I know she isn't happy. Finn used to say that she wanted us to have enough rope to hang ourselves with.

Wow. I'm actually thinking about Finn again. He's gone. He's off in Ohio pretending that he had a four-year-long psychotic break. It makes me mad every time I think about it. It's enough to make me want to swear. I haven't though, not even under my breath. I haven't broken the Oath. I still have the key. I still have my wand. All of this is real and Finn is the only one that needs help.

If I'm talking about Finn, I must really be nervous about all of this. I need to stop talking myself out of this. I'm going to go talk to them.

# 2

It's over!

Wow! I was so nervous about this but it wasn't a big deal. King Walrus just nodded yes and everyone else wished me luck. That's it. I thought it was going to be a big thing where the royalty called a trial, but it didn't happen. The whole court was there when I came to talk to them and they were all super supportive. Mama Koko was a little judgy, but she's always judgy lately. She still thinks of me as an eight-year-old. I think she *wants* me to be an eight year old! Back then she could control us.

Whatever. Who cares about what Mama Koko thinks? King Walrus is right. I saved the world. If I want to celebrate by being with Jad, then so be it! Stewart Weasel was on my side too. She's been so cool since Sashy left. I think she might be my best friend. Well, best friend outside of Lily.

I have to talk to Lily about this now. I know that this world won't matter, not really, but I still need to find her and tell her that I'm not going to be here. She's been so cool to me. She's doing so good now, Diary! She's taking this art class at the Junior College and she's getting private lessons for her violin. I've seen pictures of her teacher and he's really hot! Lily jokes about trying to seduce him, but I know she won't.

She's going to miss me. I know she is. I feel bad for taking off on her, but she doesn't need me. I've seen so many different versions of her and Lily's always doing fine. She'll find a way to move on. I just need to tell her about this without breaking the Oath. I wish my parents would move, but if I tried to convince them to move they'd know something's up.

I'm just gonna do it.

# 3

**January 20**

I don't feel like a brilliant emerald right now. I called Finn. I know how bad that sounds, Diary!

I just really needed to know what he would say about it. He's the last of the Rainbow Warriors in this world and even though he thinks we never existed, I think that some part of him knows that it's all a lie. None of us would've saved the world without Finn. I'd probably still be a pupper of Wikella without him. I might not be able to save him from the lie of adults, but he deserved to know that I was leaving.

It went about as bad as you think, Diary. He acted like I wasn't well and tried to talk me into going to a head shrink. He was going on and on so I just had to cut him off. I told him "thank you," and I apologized for leaving him behind. I told him about how Queen Nephila asked me to look after him. He felt nothing when I told him, ever after I started crying.

She doesn't understand what happened to him. She thinks that he's just busy with school. She doesn't understand that he rejected her, the court, and every experience that we had. I yelled at Finn again. I called him a traitor. I almost cursed at him. I didn't, but I thought about a bad word I wanted to call him.

Finn said, "I'll be there for you when you wake up," and hung up.

But that's Finn.

Lily didn't really get it. I ended up telling her that I was running away from home. I told her that I'd gotten in touch with Sashy and that I was going to live with her in Michigan. It probably sounded like a bad lie, but it's the best partial truth that I could come up with. I mean, Sashy went to a different world and now I'm leaving too, so in a way it's like we're both coming together, right?

Lily tried to talk me out of it. She even offered to go with me. I ended up yelling at her, telling her that I wasn't even really her friend. I came up with this lie about how I was only friends with Lily because I felt bad for her, but it didn't work. She saw through the lie and tried to get me to tell her what was really going on. I stuck with the story and hung up.

I had to get out of the house in a hurry after that. I knew she'd be coming by. It doesn't matter if she talked to mom and dad or the cops. They won't be able to find me, not now. I'm at The Gate.

I'm excited to leave, don't get me wrong. It's just that I feel a little scared now that it's really happening. If I go back now I'll have to explain where I was and why the police and my parents couldn't find me and I can't. There's no explanation that they'll believe. I guess I could tell them I got into drugs or something, but I don't know anything about that.

Why am I still worried?

I'm going to have new parents. I'll have a new best friend. Everything is going to be fine in the other world, I checked it out last night. Mom and Dad are miserable without me; so's Jad. They're going to be so happy to see me!

I shouldn't be scared or sad. This is a time to be happy! This is really happening! I'm doing it. Wish me luck, Diary!

# 4

**January 22?**

I just went through The Gate. I found shelter under the old bridge. There's graffiti here. It's a scary sight. This is where the Magicals found us all those years ago, but in this world it looks like any other bridge.

There's this arctic fox watching me. I don't think she's from the court, but you can never know. It's triggering my old instincts. That scared little girl inside me thinks Wikella's using the fox to watch me, but she's gone and dead. I'm safe now. I know that, Diary. I haven't forgotten our promise!

I don't know when I'm going to have time to write to you again, Diary. I'm heading straight to my house after this. Mom and Dad will probably freak! I can't really blame them. I died in this world. They saw their little girl in a way that no parent ever wants to see. They're going to be so happy to see me. I wonder if I'll have to talk to the police.

I think I need to hide the wand and key.

# 5

**January 23**


Mom slept with me. Dad was in the room for almost an hour. I think he was just watching us. I knew he was there though. He kept crying and muttering under his breath. He was like that when I showed up. Dad kept pinching himself. I had to pull his fingers off his skin and tell him, "You're not dreaming."

Dad just checked on me.

I'm in the living room under three blankets and Dad asked me if I needed another. The snow's coming down outside, but it feels so warm inside. It feels warmer than the home that I left. They care so much about what's going on with me. Dad would never take a day off from work.

He started a fire and he's actually cooking me a hot chocolate. It's 3 A M and he's making cocoa. I'm smiling so deep that it's squeezing tears out of my eyes, Diary! It's so wonderful to see Dad like this. He's always so distant. He's always hiding in his study and his whiskey. He thinks that I can't hear them arguing in the middle of the night.

# 6

Dad wanted to talk. It felt good to talk to him.

I know that you need to know what lies I told, and I'm going to. I've never broken a promise, have I, Diary?

I told them that I saw a light and then I woke up in the snow. I've been dead for a month in this world. They want an explanation, but none will exist. If they believe in God—if they REALLY believed in God—they'll thank Him for bringing me back to them.

I don't think they will. I don't think my parents ever really believed in God and now I'm going to know that for sure. Dad said that he's going to call the police in the morning. He said that they'll probably look for where I arrived in the snow. I told him that I showed up somewhere around the old bridge, but he didn't even know which bridge I was talking about. He asked if I would show him where I came from.

He wants to see it.

He wants to know where I really was because he doesn't believe in God.

Maybe I should feel sad that Dad's been lying to me my entire life, but I just feel vindicated. Dad knew that God and Christ were all just lies that people told themselves to feel better about the world and he never said anything because he wanted me to believe in that lie.

He's not even shaken up, not really. He's happy to see me, but he's curious as to the why. He hasn't even considered the possibility that God or angels brought me back. He probably thinks that I was drugged and kidnapped.

Wait! Am I going to have to undergo a full physical? I really don't want some old woman to touch my vagina...

# 7

I'm in my room, the police are down stairs, and I found the clothes that I'm wearing in my closet! I knew that my parents hadn't thrown anything out, but I didn't think about my clothes. There's two versions of my sweater, jeans, socks, boots, t-shirt, and bra. I'll be able to wand them away, but I can't right now! After they take me down to the station they're going to see the time clones and they're going to know that something supernatural is up! I have to hide you with the duplicate clothes.

I'll be back, Diary. I promise!

# 8

**January 26**

I'm sorry it's been three days, Diary, but I couldn't get here any sooner. You know that, right?

I told the same lie to the police and the case worker. They kept pressing me for details, but I never gave them any. I think they know that I'm lying but it doesn't matter. They can't prove that I'm actually lying. Grown ups can't see magic, so I'm fine! The worst that can happen is that they find you, but even if they do, they won't know about the secret marker. No, everything is going to be fine.

Okay, I'm doing those breathing exercises Lily told me to do. I think that this version of me, the alternate Holly, was on anxiety meds. I don't know why I didn't see that when I was dreaming about this world. I guess it was bound to happen eventually. There's so many details in another world that it's easy to miss the colors in the Rainbow of Time. Professor Owl always warned us about the dangers of jumping timelines. It probably doesn't help that I haven't done this since Wikella's death.

I don't know if I can take anxiety meds. They could help me, but taking them might break the oath. Will I be able to take them through The Gate? I don't know. Ugh! There's always problems to solve when you time jump.

I DID have a physical! It was gross and weird and there were non-doctors in the room. I lied a lot when they were asking their questions. They saw the scars. I didn't think about that and so I just had to tell them that they were scars I got as a kid. I wasn't lying, but some of the scars are strange looking. The bullbatross left a pattern that's almost a perfect star! I had to just look at them and go, "yeah, it's just a scar. I think I fell off the swing when I got that."

The physical is going to cause more problems than I thought. I think they talked to Mom and Dad about all of my injuries. I'm sure they didn't know about any of them. That's why there's a caseworker now. They're asking me a lot of questions about abuse. They want to know if my parents hit me. Someone even asked if I was pretending to be Holly Greenbay. Like...why would I?

My suicide...her suicide...

I'm just going to call the other Holly: Bolly, to avoid confusion. Bolly because she's from World B.

Bolly's suicide caught some press attention. It was a slow news cycle or something so people all over the state know that I'm supposed to be dead. Which is great; super super great! The press was there when I left downtown today. They wanted to know where I'd been. I told them the same story.

I'm supposed to be getting my phone again soon. I want to go back to school but it's still too dangerous. I think they're looking for signs of abuse, but if they check out Bolly's coroner report, they're not going to find any evidence of scars. Bolly was never a Rainbow Warrior.

It's going to be okay, Diary. I just need to talk to the Royals about the anxiety meds.

# 9

The wand and key are gone!

I checked all over.

I was so careful when I hid them. I put them under a stone under a pile of snow and the weather's been cold. The place was thick with powder, but someone had been there. Someone had pulled the stone loose and got what was inside.

It couldn't have been the arctic fox, right?

No, Wikella is dead. I promised you that I wouldn't think about her being alive, Diary. I'm going to keep that promise, but it's hard. This isn't how I thought it would go. I wanted to move here, but I didn't want to lose the wand and key. Queen Nephila needs the wand and key back.

I can watch The Gate entrance everyday until I see them again.

I'm tired from all the crying, Diary. I'll try to write more later.

# 10

**February 3**

I can only stay by The Gate for about thirty minutes. Then the cold gets to be too much and I have to head home. I saw the arctic fox again today. I know it probably doesn't mean anything, but she keeps looking right at me. I think I should name the fox. In her winter coat, I want to name her Katherine. I wish I could see what she looks like in the fall. I keep thinking that I should bring her something to eat, but foxes can be trouble. There's some chicken farms not too far from The Gate.

I know that I should've written more, but I got a phone. So many people are reaching out to me. Yes, some of them are the press. I've been telling everyone the same lie, but I don't have to tell you if I repeat a lie, right? I don't know. I wish I could talk to Judge Cobra.

They want me to do an interview over Zoom. It sounds so boring, but it could help me get back to school. That's really all I want right now. I've been through three more physicals. They keep poking at my scars. They've told me that they believe me about the scar tissue being old, which is good, but I don't think they believe me overall.

Lily and I are best friends again. She came over and hugged me and she cried for like an hour. My leaving was hard for her. I've had to spend a lot of time just hugging her and reassuring her that I'm alive and that everything is going to be back to normal now. She wanted to know why I did it.

I don't know why Bolly killed herself, but I know why I would.

I told Lily that I did it because I was off my meds and not thinking straight. I told her that I didn't want to live without Jad.

She got mad at me for saying that. Lily kept talking about how much she loved me and how much it hurt that I didn't feel the same way. But I love Lily. I've always loved Lily. It's just that there's always been this separation between us.

I met her after Wikella was defeated. She never got to know me before all the battles. I've always been a shy sad kid to her. She never got to see me when I was just happy to be alive. I liked that about her. I liked that Lily wasn't asking me if I was okay because as far as she knew, I was. She never saw me as someone who missed her friends. She didn't know that I was dealing with the death of four of them. And thanks to the Oath I never had to tell her.

Sashy taking off gave us something to talk about. I kind of talked about the trauma a little, but there was so much I could never tell Lily. I liked the distance it gave us. I liked that I had a friend that wasn't connected to the Rainbow Warriors and Wikella. I liked being with someone that didn't look at every animal with suspicion.

There's more to our relationship than that. There are things that I haven't told Lily about, but I've already told you about it, Diary, so I don't need to talk about it again, right? Lily is my normal human friend. It's important that we're just happy and chill with each other, but things just keep getting weirder.

I don't like how Sashy's disappearance took our surface deep friendship from us. I don't like that Lily knows about my panic attacks and how I think that attacks are coming for me when Wikella is dead. I liked it better when we'd just gossip about stuff at school and I could just chill and read her stories. I miss her writing. I hate that she gave up on it just because she talked to her cousin in college. That guy's fudge with nuts.

When I met Lily, I was her hero. I saved her from those cheerleader wannabes. I was there to stand up for her when she was just the awkward new girl and that meant I got to have a best friend. She was the only person I ever saved without my wand. She always thought I was cool. I loved seeing that in her eyes and I can't tell her that.

Part of the reason I came here was to see that look in her eyes again. But I don't think she ever will. She's so mad at me for killing myself, but I didn't actually kill myself. That was Bolly. She's mad at me for being someone that I'm not.

It's so frustrating. Why can't she just be like Mom and Dad. All they ever do is tell me how happy they are that I'm in their lives again. I can get whatever I want for dinner and I don't have to do chores. It's like the home life that I've always wanted.

I have so much more to tell you, Diary, but I'm getting tired.

# 11

**February 4**

So...Jad did reach out to me. He messaged me pretty soon after the press was calling me Lazarus Girl. That's what they're calling me, by the way, Lazarus Girl. Even though Mom and Dad didn't jump to the God angle, the press did. They did one of those things where they walk around and ask normal people about my story and a bunch of people kept calling it a miracle.

Oh, and get this! That burn mark around my ankle, where Destrus dragged me into the hallows, people are saying that's where an angel dragged me out of hell. A bunch of people think that my scars are from where the demons were torturing me. It sucks that everyone thinks I went to hell, but I did kill myself.

I think that they want me to talk about how great it is that God's giving me this second chance. Like I'm just going to be a super Christian because I died and came back to life. But I don't remember what happened to me; by my story at any rate. Obviously, I know why I'm here and what happened, but my story is just that I saw a white light and then I woke up in the snow.

That's right! I still need to get rid of the time cloned clothes. I better just burn them. I think I'm going to ask Mom and Dad to get me a whole new wardrobe. I'm tired of wearing all of this drab stuff. I don't feel sad and in pain anymore. I have everything I've ever wanted now. Well, I will soon enough. I just wish that Lily wasn't being such a bitter cookie.

I wish that Lily would try harder to see things from my way. I killed myself because I was in pain and she keeps acting like I should feel bad because it hurt her. I never realized how selfish she was before. I was so sad that I killed myself, so why does she keep laying on the guilt?! It's not right for her to treat me this way.

I'm all over the place. Sorry, Diary.

Okay, so let's talk about the big stuff: Jad.

Jad's first message almost word for word:

*I'm so glad you're back Holly. I know that I was mean to you before you disappeared. I'm sorry. I'm so sorry that I looked the other way when you came into the hall and that I would leave a table when you sat down next to me. I'm sorry that I told Layton that you were a girl in my math class. You're my friend. You were always my friend.*

*I liked you as my friend. I know that you wanted us to be something more, but I couldn't. I was scared. I used to think that I was scared of losing you as a friend, but now I know that's a lie.*

*Do you remember what you were like in first grade, before you started hanging out with Sasha and Finn and them all the time? You were so happy. You'd run around the playground smiling all the time. You gave me a handful of daisies once in kindergarten. Do you remember that? I used to think that I was going to grow up and ask you to marry me. I don't know what happened to you.*

*I've heard that you have a lot of scars and that you don't really remember how you got them. I feel like a fool for not speaking up. I saw the smile fade from your lips when we grew up. I saw the glimmer in your eyes grow dim and I never told anyone.*

*I told people about it when you were gone. I started seeing a therapist. She's a really nice woman. I know you hate your head shrink—I still don't think you should call her that—but mine spends a lot of time listening to me and has a lot of kind things to say. She helps me.*

*This was a very roundabout way of saying that I was afraid to make you sad, but I did anyway. I kept thinking about how ironic that was, but it didn't help me after you left. I missed you, Holls. I missed seeing you at school. Even before you went away, I missed talking to you outside Yearbook.*

*I hope you're still talking to Lily, or that you started talking to her after you got back. She's a really good friend. Remember when you said that you're not sure if you can ever love anyone like how you loved Sasha? I hope you can find a way to love Lily that way. She really cares about you. We became friends because of Lily. So what if she quit Future Authors Club, at least she's doing something with her creativity. Did Lily tell you that she started drawing comics again after you left? They're really good.*

*You know, you could've kept coming to Future Authors. We all liked having you there. Even though you were really self conscious about your stories, I thought they were cool. I liked that you didn't have to write about sad teenagers or big fights. I liked King Walrus and Queen Nephila. It cracked me up to think about a walrus and a big spider [f-word].*

*You know, every time I swear I think of you. I've never met anyone who doesn't curse. I think that it makes people nervous. It kind of makes everyone feel judged. But I never got the impression that you were judging us for swearing. You honestly kind of looked jealous. You looked that way about a lot of things.*

*Sorry I'm going on for so long. I wrote you when you disappeared. It was helping me cope with your loss. I guess I can just write you now, is that okay?*

*I missed you. I hope we can meet again soon.*

I thought about just telling him to come over, but I didn't know if that was a good idea or not. I called Lily over but she just wanted to talk about my death and her feelings about my death and her feelings about my feelings about her death and on and on. Like, I know that me dying was a big deal, but I'm alive now and she's really bumming me out. It's like she wants me to feel as sad as she did when she saw me dead. It's not like she saw me dead, anyway. Mom and Dad found my body and they're doing okay. They're moving on, why can't she?!

Ugh! I have to do this video interview soon.

# 12

Fudge! I messed up. I talked about Lily!

I don't know how this happened. They were asking all these really easy questions to answer. They talked about God. They asked me if I believed before and if I believed now. I don't but I did that thing where I look away and go, "I'm just not sure anymore." That feels like something someone would say if they were in my position. They kind of talked to me about angels and out of body experiences. They asked if I was researching it and I was like, "Why would I do more homework?" That made them laugh. I don't want to sound too smart.

Anyway, they asked to see my scars. I showed them the star and the hand print. I guess those two got a lot of press coverage. Someone at the police station must've leaked the photos. I guess it could've only been one of four people, so they found them and they lost their job. I know I shouldn't feel bad about that, but if I hadn't come here, they wouldn't have leaked those photos. Professor Owl always told us not to cry about butterflies. I'm not.

I still don't know how they got me to talk about Lily. They asked me something like, "how's life been since you've been back? Is everyone being nice to you?"

I talked about how cool Mom and Dad were and how I wanted to go back to school. I thought that maybe talking about it online could pressure them to hurry up and put me back into school. They asked about my friends and then I just started bitterly complaining about Lily. I didn't say her name, but it's pretty obvious that I was talking about her. She's going to see the interview, or she's already seen it.

I didn't say anything too bad. All I said was that she seemed to want to make everything about her. I died and she wants to talk about her pain. I was feeling so bad that I ended my life but she wants to make me feel bad for leaving her, for giving up on life. I already made the decision to kill myself, doesn't that mean I felt bad enough as it is? I'm still kind of mad at her, but I definitely shouldn't have talked about it in the interview. The reporters took my side though. They said, "Sometimes selfish people are like that, they just want everything to be about them." It was nice to finally hear someone take my side about this, because Lily hasn't since I got back.

She better apologize to me. I'm going to forgive her because I'm a good person, but I need to hear that apology before I can move on.

# 13

**February 7**

I realized I didn't tell you everything that happened with Jad.

I was waiting for Lily to give me advice, but she didn't. I tried bringing up Jad, she just changed topics. One time she was even like, "I don't think that we should talk about him." When I brought it up again she didn't want to hear it. So I was like, "Why do you have a problem with Jad and me getting together?"

She said, "I don't. I just don't think that you should be thinking about the guy that broke your heart so bad that you jammed a [f-word] blade into your wrist!"

That made me mad. I started yelling about how I didn't kill myself because of him and how she doesn't know anything about what I'm going through or why I did it. Then Lily wanted me to talk about it some more and I didn't know what to say. That was like two days ago. I wanted to write to you, Diary, but there's just so much going on and I was more interested in my conversation with Jad.

I started talking to him. I feel like posting our entire conversations here, but it would hurt my hand to rewrite it all. I know that you said that I have to write in here for you to read it, Diary, so I'm gonna be good and try to summarize things.

Reading Jad's message was strange. He was talking about this person that he thought I was, but it was just this mask that I put on. Bolly basically has the same past as me except my time as a Rainbow Warrior was a dream or a game of pretend. It feels deceptive to get praise for writing about King Walrus and Queen Nephila. I didn't make them, I was just using something familiar to write so I could be with Lily and Jad.

It was weird how he saw my smile fade. I didn't know that happened in elementary. Maybe it was just Bolly losing her smile, but the same probably happened to me. I chose this world for a reason. I needed Bolly to be like me or it wouldn't have felt right to take her place. It's strange to think of young Jad watching me from afar. He talked about marrying me.

I told Jad that I hadn't been writing. If I went back to Future Authors, I could go back to my old adventures, but I never really liked writing about the Rainbow Warriors. I tried to write short stories about the court and the Royals because I knew them so well. They've been like a family to me. It's been more than a week since I've seen them now. I really miss them.

Jad got back to me about my lying.

He said that if I couldn't tell anyone he understood. He also said that lying to a therapist probably kept my time from being productive. I think he wants me to try therapy again. But the thing is that Bolly killed herself, not me. I shouldn't need to see a therapist when I didn't do anything wrong. I know that he only means well, but he really doesn't know what he's talking about. No one does. Maybe that's the whole problem with living with all of these secrets: every bit of advice I get is coming from a lie.

I have to work so hard to convert all of the advice into something that I can use.

Jad wants to meet soon. The last message he sent me, he asked if he could come to visit me, but I don't know if he should. Mom and Dad would probably freak if they saw him with me. I think they kind of blame him for Bolly's death.

I wish everyone knew about Wikella and Sashy and Finn and the Rainbow Warriors. If they knew about how we saved the world as kids then it would be easier to tell them about why I killed myself. I mean, Bolly. Bolly probably couldn't cope with the hallucinations. She lost touch with what was real. Besides that, Wikella and the Troops of Evil were scary. I spent half a summer as her pupper. I cursed at Mom. I broke the car. I stole Dad's whiskey. They think that I did that, but I didn't.

I need a better lie than, "I saw a light and woke up in the snow." There's too much of my past that I want to talk about. But that's a trap. Captain Alligator always told us that a truth that causes pain is told for your conscience.

I'm so tired of the lies.

# 14

**February 9**

Reading that last entry, I'm like, what?

Why was I so sad?

It's only been two days later, but I think these anxiety meds are helping my mood. My stomach kind of hurts, but that's supposed to be kind of normal. My period is probably going to start next week and I think I might actually puke. It feels that bad.

But that's like the only bad thing. It's like some magic drug that takes away the bad. I saw my therapist yesterday, but it was boring. I told the same kind of lies that I always tell. I know that I wanted to come up with a better lie, but it's not going to work. Any lie that I come up with needs to have something to prove the truth of it. I can't explain my scars.

I guess someone hacked into the police database and found pictures of Bolly's corpse. She didn't have my scars. They know something's up with me. Lots of people are saying that I'm not even Holly, but I have the same dental records. I have the same funny DNA.

I almost swore again. It's getting harder not to swear, especially now that I don't have the wand and key.

Oh! I can't believe I almost forgot about this!

I met a boy. Well, I didn't meet him so much as he met me. I think he lives by The Gate because he came to talk to me when I was waiting for it to open. His name is Brandon Waters. I don't really like the name, but he's got a really interesting face. He almost looks like a lizard and half his lip is larger than the other half. I keep staring at him. I don't know.

I'm pretty sure he's into me because this morning he

said that my snow cap was cute. Boys never call my clothes cute. Mom and Dad obvi spent lots on my new threads, but a compliment is a big deal. That means he's into me.

I don't know if I'm into him. I mean, obviously I'm into Jad, but it's just kind of nice to meet someone and know that they like me how I am. I'm not going to do anything with Brandon, it's just nice to talk to him.

He offered to wait with me at The Gate and I just kind of had to accept. If he's going to be there when I'm there, I'm gonna have to come back later. The Gate isn't going to open if a norm is watching it.

Brandon's really into music. He knows all this stuff about bands that I've never heard. I didn't believe him when he said he liked punk music. He looks super boring. No mohawk, nothing like that. I called him out on it and he started listing all of these bands and guitarists like it proved he knew what he was talking about, but he could've been making it all up.

I don't know, Diary. Do you think that I'm being mean to Brandon? If he likes me and I'm going to be with Jad, then every time I'm talking to him it's kind of like I'm hurting him more later on.

Again, it's not like I even WANT anything to happen with Brandon. It's just that he doesn't know that I died. He isn't trying to talk about therapy or medication like I don't know what I'm doing with my own brain. He doesn't ask me if I'm okay every time I see him and it's really cool. I get to just listen to him talk about add 13 chords on his guitar and not really know what he's talking about.

Maybe I could be in a band with him and it would like just be our thing. The last time I tried to play an instrument was flute and I was horrible at that. It would be different now because the Troops of Evil wouldn't keep me from practicing. I could actually try to do music this time. Brandon had me sing a little and he says that it was deep. That's bad right? Girls are supposed to have high voices.

# 15

Jad is coming over!

I don't know what to wear. I'm kind of freaking but in a good way. I got this new top that's like green and purple with these little frills. It's not really a winter top but I think it looks cute and I want to try to do my eyes to match. I already have the perfect lip gloss. I wish I could show you how cute I look now, Diary. You wouldn't even recognize me!

# 16

Okay, Diary, I'm going to write about every single moment because I want to remember it exactly as it happened. I'm even gonna try to write about the bad stuff, but I promise there's not that much.

So I put on that green and purple top and my makeup wasn't perfect. I got some smudges and clumps. I tried to fix them with Yoot vids but it was too much. I ended up just leaving it kind of whatever.

I didn't tell Mom and Dad about Jad coming over. Every time I go out to The Gate or even to the grocery store they give me my space, which is totally cool. Mom used to give me the third degree whenever she was home. Now they just tell me to have fun. This time I think Mom knew I was going out to meet someone so she gave me sixty bucks. That doesn't even sound like Mom, right?!

I met Jad by the bleachers at Elmswood Park. There wasn't a game and almost no one was there. The powder was mostly fresh and the sun was just starting to come down. When it started setting the whole baseball field lit up like fire. It was perfect!

Jad brought so many whozits and whatzits that he could barely walk. He had this whole box of stuff that we'd done together. He'd kept the ticket stubs from the movies and from when we went to support Lily when she was a black shirt for Wizard of Oz. He showed me the cracked shell I found when we went to the lake and it still had the glitter glue he used at Lily's house. Jad also brought two blankets, one for the bleachers and the other for us. Well, he said it was for me, but I'm like never cold.

We sat on the bleachers for maybe an hour. Jad was just talking about the old days, mostly back when he, Lily, Madelyn, and I were thick as thieves. He brought up Future Authors a lot. I think he knew that I didn't really want to go back to the club, but he told me that it wouldn't be a big deal because it would mostly be us just hanging out. I asked if he'd been writing and he lit up. He had. He had a whole three-ring binder full of short stories he'd been working on since we'd talked last. Jad said that he tried to write about my death, but all he wrote were those letters to me.

I wanted to see them, but he was super guarded about it.

The setting sun started shining in our eyes so we moved to sit under a tree away from the road. We were basically alone and it was breezy so close to the creek. I told a lie to Jad, but I think you'd approve. We sat down on the blanket and even though I had the whole blanket over me, I told him, "I'm still cold." That's when he got inside and we shared the blanket! I was so close to him that I could feel his breath on my cheek. He'd brushed his teeth and chewed white mints. I know because I could smell them on his breath!

He started holding my hand and swallowing a lot. I thought he was going to kiss me but then he looked away and said, "You know, Lily's worried about you."

It was so hard to not just scream at him! I didn't want to think about Lily, but she was his friend too, so I needed to listen. I guess the two of them got closer after Bolly left.

"Lily says you're different."

"What do you say?"

He nodded. "You're definitely different."

I didn't like how that sounded so I got really sour and told him, "thanks."

Then Jad brushed my hair behind my ear and said, "in a good way."

I almost died! My heart was pounding. I really thought he was going to kiss me. I leaned in like, "go for it!" but he kept talking.

"I think you're happier. Not like in grade school, but more mature. You were like a little girl then. Now...I don't know. I've never seen you like this."

I tried to kiss him then. I didn't care that he was trying to have this conversation about me, I just needed to kiss him. I'd been waiting so long for the two of us to get together. Everything I'd done had been to feel him against me and now that he was snuggling with me, I couldn't keep waiting.

And Jad pulled his head away!

"I started dating Fifi."

Can you believe it, Diary? I actually died! I literally killed myself and he started dating Fifi! Ugh! I hate her name. I hate writing her name. She's such a slut! Everyone at school knows it! She's been dress coded like a hundred times. Who wears spaghetti strings when it's snowing outside? Fifi, that's who.

I felt so humiliated. I thought that after I'd died he would've known how important I was, but he ended up kissing Fifi anyway! It was disgusting. It was like he'd shoved me back into my own world but so much worse. I wanted to curl up and die, but I didn't. I stayed there and when I grabbed his hand, he squeezed it back.

I asked Jad, "After I?"

"Yeah."

I fought back the tears. I didn't want him to think that I couldn't handle this.

Jad talked about how my death had hurt him and made him really vulnerable and even though he didn't say it, Fifi took advantage of him. I wasn't there for him. Lily was wigging out herself, and when Fifi saw how hurt Jad was, she scooped him up. He says it happened like a week after the fact, but maybe not even that. No surprise from the Slut Queen herself.

When Jad was talking about him and Fifi, he kept pausing to see if I was going to flip. I thought I was going to but I focused on his hand in mine. If he was Fifi's boy, then why was he holding my hand? He loved me. He always loved me. I knew he did, but with everything else going on in my life I didn't let myself believe it. All of that was going to change.

Jad broke up with Fifi after I got back. I guess they tried to make things work for a few days, but Jad ended it. He told her, "I don't know how I feel anymore," and broke things off. I would've paid good money to watch that slut cry her eyes out.

After that he kept talking about his feelings and how everything had been so confusing since I came back and I was barely listening. I kept leaning into him. Our chests were right up against each other under that blanket. I could feel every breath he took. I could feel his heart pounding against mine. He smelled so good, like walnuts and caramel. Finally, I couldn't take it anymore and I did it, Diary!

I kissed Jad!

We were at a weird angle, so I kind of kissed him on the cheek first. He was a little confused but he didn't move away. We stayed there kissing for like five minutes. Neither of us moved, not even to part our lips. Some sparrows flew by and we drew back and Jad couldn't keep his eyes off me.

"I love you, Jad."

He closed his eyes and I could see this pain and confusion on his brow.

"Say it, Jad."

"I love you too."

After that it was like some switch in his brain got flicked. He started kissing my cheek and stroking my hair. He kept telling me that he loved me and he laid me down and we made out until the sun was gone.

It was so perfect and wonderful that I felt like I was going to cry.

When it started getting hard to see him we talked again. I wanted to know why it took him so long to tell me how he felt.

"Because of you. I didn't want to hurt you. Things must be hard with you coming back to life. I'm sure all of this is overwhelming. Besides, I keep hearing things in the media."

"What kind of things?"

"People are saying that you're not really Holly. They say that someone else showed up to impersonate you, that you have all of these scars because you were abused and you escaped."

"I'm Holly, Jad."

"I know that now. You remember everything we did together. You even remember the stories you wrote. You remember them better than I do. Every time you talk about the Magicals, you add new details in a way that an impersonator never would. I know it's you now, Holls, but I still feel bad."

It was hard to see his face in the dim light, but I could hear the pain in his voice. He felt really guilty about making out with me. Earlier that hesitation might have hurt, but I knew just how bad he wanted me. I felt it when he was on top of me! Please don't think too bad of me, Diary. I'm not a little girl anymore. I'm an adult and I wanna be with him. I want to love him with everything that I am and he wants that too.

Anyway, Jad wanted to wait a little before kissing me because of everything that I was going through and because of what had happened with Fifi. When he was walking me home he told me about how Fifi still had feelings for him. He thought she would move on, because let's face it, she will. But because she hasn't found a new guy to use yet he feels bad about her. I think he wanted to wait for Fifi to find a new man, but I don't want to wait.

I've waited too long for Jad. Maybe I've waited my whole life for this. He wants to try and keep things slow and wait a little before telling anyone. I can do that just as long as we can keep meeting up and kissing for an hour.

I can still feel his lips on mine, Diary!

**February 10**

I feel like I keep forgetting to tell you things, but it's not because I don't still care about you, Diary. It's just that things are finally happening for me. I don't have to be this sad girl who hides her beauty and cries all the time. I can be happy. I know that you're happy for me, Diary. I can feel it in my toes, just like you said I could.

Today was a big day like most every day has been. First of all, they're finally letting me go back to school! It's gonna be so great walking hand in hand with Jad. I can't wait to see the look on Fifi's face when she realizes that Jad and I are together. Well, I'm gonna have to wait, but it's gonna come and it'll be so sweet!

The press hasn't really done any more reports about me lately. There was this news segment on some channel no one watches about how I'm probably an identical twin since I have the same DNA, finger prints, and dental records. Some people think that I faked my death and they're talking about exhuming my corpse, but Mom and Dad keep telling those people "no." I'm back and that's all that they care about. I think the people that really love me only care about that. That's gotta be why Lily's been such a bitter cookie.

I had to go to her house today, because I'm over the drama. She took a sick day, but when I got to her place with chicken soup, she didn't even have a sore throat. But, Diary, Lily looked pretty bad. She wasn't wearing her makeup and her hair was a mess. I combed it and braided it. I wanted to talk about fashion stuff, but she had all this drama going on in her life.

She told me sorry, which was good. I know that she doesn't really love me now, but it's good to know that she at least cares about what I think. I didn't really talk about why Lily went silent because I thought it was pretty obvious. Lily was sucking lemons because I talked about her on "national TV," but first of all I didn't even do the interview on national TV. I talked to a small Christian website and that interview got spread around. No one even speculated about who my bitter friend was, they just used it to try and attack my character like every other news segment about me. It's always "we can't trust her," and "what do we even know about this girl?" They only ever bring me up to talk about God or modern science and identity theft. I'm getting emails again about doing interviews. One of them is this makeup vlogger I've been watching lately: Jemmie G. Should I do it, Diary?

But Lily apologized for going silent and that's what's important here. She felt really bad for turning her back on me, but she thought I didn't care about her anymore; which is so not true. I always made time for Lily and her problems before I died. Things are just different now because all of these things are happening for me now.

Lily knows it because she was talking about how our dynamic was changing and how she needed to accept that. Also, she admitted that she wasn't sure if I was even me anymore. She brought up my new look, which is like, what?! She was the one who's been talking me into putting more effort in my appearance since spring of eighth grade! Now that I finally am, she's acting like it's proof that I'm not me.

I told her, "I'm just trying to be happy. I'm letting go of the pain and the guilt like everyone's always telling me to do."

That eased some of her fears, but we still had to talk about me and my motivations for a good hour after that. She doesn't really get why I do any of these interviews. It's not about the attention, I just think that the best way to get people to leave me alone is to be transparent. If they see me they won't wonder about me, right?

Going over to Lily's house wasn't just about me, either. The whole time Lily was waiting for her mom to take off. When she did, she came clean about what's really been going on with her. Lily stayed home because she felt guilty.

"I'm like a bunny putting on their winter coat. I hop around the warren and think it's strange that everyone is still brown and cream colored, until I go outside and find a green world without snow. I remember that I'm the one who's changed."

I thought that was pretty deep from her and once I heard it I started to cry. That's what I'd been going through too, but I didn't know who I could talk about that. I can never talk to anyone though, not really. Without you, Diary, I don't know what I would've done.

Sorry, I just kind of had this huge mood swing. Blame my PMS, right? I hate that. I hate that boys never have to deal with this.

So Lily's big secret is that she isn't a virgin anymore. Yeah, and it's probably with who you think.

It happened after I disappeared. She had been thinking about trying to kiss her violin teacher for awhile, but every time she imagined kissing him she could see him telling her that he was too old. So Lily got it in her head that things were only going to happen if she touched his crotch. She was kind of trying to talk herself into it before I left. After I did, she was crying a lot. Then one day he put his arm around her to comfort her and she made her move.

She said that they used a condom and that was really weird to me. Did this guy already have a condom? Did Lily buy the condom? I wanted to ask her about it, but I couldn't. I think it proves that she's still keeping things from me. I'm obvi doing likewise, but I have to because of the Oath.

I keep thinking about how this 22 year-old man had sex with a sixteen-year-old girl. He's probably done this before. Lily says that it was her decision, but he's an older man who's probably been with lots of girls before. If he was seducing her and grooming her, would she even know?

I wish I still had my wand. I could find him and bring him

to justice. He's a sexual predator, right? I know that he isn't part of the Troops of Evil, but he's still evil! Queen Nephila always told me that heroism isn't about the wands, it's about my spirit. If I can stop him, I should.

I don't know. Lily was really nervous about telling me about this stuff, but she said that she needed to tell me because she couldn't tell her therapist. She was too worried that the head shrink would come after her violin teacher. She said that after I came back they stopped hooking up. That sounds like they've had sex more than once, right?

I guess she had violin lessons yesterday and she almost did something again. She just said, "we started kissing," but I think how she said it meant something more. It sounded like she was going to do it, but she stopped him. At least he stopped, I guess. I don't know.

So if I still had my powers I could've seen this coming. Even if I didn't, I could erase him or send him to the Crystal Prison. Judge Cobra would be on my side, right? I wish I could talk to the Magicals about this. I know that Lily told me because she thinks that I won't stop him, but I can. Even without my powers I can still do the right thing by reporting him.

Those who allow evil have evil in their hearts.

If I told Lily to report him, she'd be mad at me. People always bullied me for being a goody goody, but this is different, right? He's twenty-two!

# 18

**February 15**

I did the makeup interview with Jemmie G. For the most part, it was me talking about high school. She wasn't trying to trap me or anything, it was really chill. She talked about how she had tried to kill herself when she was my age. It was her Mom that really pushed her over the edge. She used to grab Jemmie by the hair and throw her into the wall. There was more too, but it was too much for her. At one point she said, "it was worse for my brother," and something about the tone made it really heavy.

Jemmie couldn't talk about it before now because her mom was coming up on parole, but it was denied. I told Jemmie that it was good that she reported her mother, but I don't think she did because my comment haunted her. I'm really glad there was a moderator there to keep the conversation moving after I made that mistake.

They wanted me to talk about school and my suicide. Well, they didn't mention the suicide explicitly, but they talked around it.

I knew that I needed to talk about more than Jad, but I didn't exactly lie so I'm not sure if I need to tell you about it, Diary. I'm going to anyway, though.

# 19

Sorry, Jad called me and we went out. He saw my interview on Jemmie G and he was really worried about me. He had a lot of homework to do and it was really cold out, but we met for about an hour. I'm glad we did. It felt so good to have him hold me and kiss the tears off my face. I think this is how girls are supposed to cry, with a man there to hold her and kiss the tears off her face. I feel so light and warm. He was so warm, Diary.

Sorry, you probably don't want to hear about this, but there's nothing wrong with what I'm doing. Jad and I are in love. Everything we're doing is natural and beautiful and you don't need to worry about me. I haven't broken the Oath. I've kept all of my promises to you.

Jad still doesn't want us to be a couple at school. I know it's because of Fifi, but I don't want to fight with him about it so I just said, "okay." That's the only lie I told him.

Okay, fine! I also told him that his new jacket looked good on him. It's a weird color and it doesn't feel good on my arm. It's like an old man's jacket.

Anyway, going back to the interview, it's kind of the same stuff that I already talked about. Right, Diary? I just really don't want to feel bad right now. Things are going well. The interview was a lot and meeting Jad filled up that hole. So I'm just going to go to sleep, okay? Goodnight, Diary.

# 20

Seriously, Diary?! You just have to know about this now, huh?! Why can't you just let me sleep? At least let me go to sleep!

# 21

**February 16**

You're being so annoying.

Fine, I'll tell you all about the interview. But after that you need to let me sleep.

They were asking me about school and my suicide. They wanted to know what high school was like for me. I told them all about how I lost all of my friends going into freshman year. My parents were really mad at me. Mom had started her affair and Dad was working at the gas station and I was really alone.

I kept trying to make new friends, but only Finn and Sashy would talk to me. Finn was trying to make new friends too and it made Sashy feel like we didn't care about her. I told them about how Sashy stuffed a bunch of cake into her face and sobbed at her birthday party. It's just one of those moments that stuck with me I guess.

I couldn't make friends, not really. Someone would sit by me and then invite me to sit with their friends. We'd talk about shows and bands and it was fine, but someone would talk about having a drink or swiping a lip gloss from Target and I would tell them it's wrong. They said that I should sit at the Christian table, but I knew God was a lie.

I had to switch schools going into eighth grade. Finn was in the basketball team, so he stayed. For awhile, it was just Sashy and me. We spent like every day that summer together and she was doing better, but I needed friends outside of her. That's when I became friends with Lily.

Lily was always really cool. I'd come to talk to her and she'd bring up all of this stuff about her old school or Max's latest reason for being grounded. I could just forget about everything and have a friend. Lily got really popular and even though her friends weren't really my friends, she'd invite me to go to the movies with them and things like that.

I had to tell Jemmie G about Sashy disappearing. I really wanted to tell them the truth. I know that I took the Oath, but I don't have the key or the wand. It shouldn't matter anymore, right? Why am I still keeping the Oath if I can't see the Magicals?!

Sorry, I'm just really mad at you right now, Diary! I know that the Magicals are my friends and that they're only looking out for me, but I can't see them and it's hard for me. I was starting to wonder if you ever even existed when you kept me from going to sleep.

Anyway, I didn't break the Oath. I told them about Sashy leaving, like she just ran away from home. I guess to everyone else, that's what happened to her. They never found her body. Her parents never properly mourned. I told them about how her mom grabbed me by the arms at the wake and begged me to tell her what happened to her daughter. I kept my Oath then. I kept my Oath when it meant that her mom could sleep knowing her daughter wasn't being raped or tortured. Okay. I'm still on your side. I'm still a Rainbow Warrior, okay? I'm just tired.

What else do I need to tell you so that I'll sleep?

Right, the suicide. So I told them about how my morals kept me from making friends. I talked about meeting Jad and how cool he was. I told them about falling in love and how he scorned me for a popular bimbo and then it was weird. Well, it didn't happen right away. The moderator wanted to ask about my no swearing policy.

She was like, "if you don't swear, why do you call Barbie a bimbo?"

Oh, Barbie was my fake name for Fifi. I used fake names for everyone.

Anyway, I was like, "what? Bimbo isn't a curse word, and neither is slut."

The moderator got mad but Jemmie G calmed her down. It was like, you're there to keep us from going off topic, cool your tits.

Anyway, I told them about Jad breaking my heart, which was weird because we're dating now, and I was like, "I felt like the only rabbit in white in the middle of summer." And I think they got it. Jemmie G said that was a great way of putting how it feels to be isolated and excluded. I tried to say that Lily came up with it, but they kind of cut me off to wrap things up. They asked if I was going to start streaming or do a podcast or something. I don't know if I should.

Can I sleep now, Diary? Will you leave me alone?

# 22

**February 17**

Lily is being a bitter cookie again!

She's all mad at me for stealing her idea and talking about it in the interview like it was my own, but I didn't. Why is she like this?!

Don't think I just sat there and took it though. I told her that what she was doing with her violin teacher was wrong. I told her that it was statutory rape and that she should report him and then she turned things around on me.

She said, "That's why you didn't have any friends in seventh grade! You were always judging people! If you can't let people live their lives and make their own mistakes then you're going to be alone for the rest of yours!"

"I'm not going to be alone! Jad is my boyfriend, okay! He likes that I'm honest. He likes that I care about what people think. He said that I was the bravest person he knew, but it's good to know that I'm just a hypocrite to you!"

That kind of shook her. She calmed down and asked how long I'd been seeing him and things like that. She was biting her tongue, so I made her ask what she was thinking. "Don't you think it's wrong to hook up with the guy that made you kill yourself?"

"He didn't make me kill myself, okay! It's not just about him. I just...I felt alone. I felt like no one was ever going to know who I was, like I was never going to belong!"

"Like a white rabbit in the middle of summer?"

You see what she does, Diary! She's always like that! She always has to say something clever. She's not as smart as she thinks she is, especially since she's willing to have sex with someone who's way older than her. He's a funny sexual predator, Lily, like come on! She told me she was in love! I guess she didn't want to tell me before because she thought that love would make me relapse and kill myself again or something. But what Jad and I have is a hundred percent different. It's real and it's something that she'll never have.

In the middle of our fight, Lily had to go to the bathroom. She made me promise to not go home. I almost left right there. She was so jealous and so full of herself. Lily just thinks so high of herself and I'm just like this little toy dog that she keeps on a leash and now that people all over the world are talking about how pretty I am, she's jealous. She's jealous of me and Jad too, I could see it on her face. But I stayed. I kept my promise to her.

When Lily got back, she was contrite. She told me that she was just worried that all of this attention was too much too fast. I'm doing interviews and dating Jad and in three days I'm going back to school and she's worried that it's going to be too much. But I'm fine. I told her I'd be fine too. You know that I'm not lying. You know when I'm lying and when I'm telling the truth. I wish Lily could do the same. She's such a bitter bitter cookie!

# 23

**February 18**

I talked to Brandon for like two hours today. I wasn't flirting either!

It was just like, the two of us talking about music and stuff. He brought me some music to listen to. He wanted to know if I was a fan of Linkin Park. I recognized some but I'd never really paid attention. He wanted to listen to a whole album, so we did. We were sharing headphones but he didn't touch my hand or anything like Jad would've done. I'm not even interested in him like that.

It was cool listening to music with him and talking about how it made me feel. I guess he really likes the lead singer because Brandon talked about him a lot. He killed himself. When he first started talking about how Chester took his life I got really nervous. I wondered if he knew I was the Lazarus Girl and he was trying to get me to talk about it, but he just kept talking about Chester. He actually teared up while talking about him.

The first time I saw Jad cry was when I confessed to him. I've never seen a boy cry just from talking about music. It was kind of cool. He didn't even apologize for it. He was okay with crying in front of me. I don't think he was ashamed of it. I wish I could cry like that, without any shame. Every time I cry, I can feel Mom frowning at me, or hear Dad tell me to smile because no one can smile and cry at the same time. Even when I'm alone at The Gate I feel like someone's looking at me.

I've been writing to you in front of The Gate lately. I need to go there twice a day. I guess I could stop going in the morning, but Brandon's a good friend. I hope he gets a girlfriend soon because I don't want to have to tell him that I have a boyfriend.

I'd say that he already has a girlfriend, but I don't even need to ask. He's not cute. His face is kind of pinched in and he's got these odd shaped lips. Like the bottom right side of his lip is bigger than the rest of his lips and they're kind of thick anyway. I feel bad for Brandon, but maybe he can find a really nice fat girlfriend or something. I think for someone like that, they'd be really happy to be with Brandon.

Anyway, do you think I should talk to Lily about Brandon? I feel like she'll just try to take the moral high ground with me, but I'm not interested in dating him anyway. Maybe it'll be better for Lily if she thinks I'm just as bad as her. She's still being a bitter cookie about everything. I don't even know.

Oh, I guess some people online turned on me because I said God was a lie, but he is and everyone knows it. Just because I saw a white light and woke doesn't even prove that God exists. I appeared in this world because I'm a Rainbow Warrior. They can't accept what they can't see so they make up this fiction about God and Christ and Satan. I guess it's just too hard for people to admit that they're evil all by themselves.

I used to wonder why Wikella could corrupt and tempt adults so easily. I don't wonder about that anymore.

# 24

I talked to Jad about Brandon. He said it was cool that I had a guy friend. I'm so glad I'm with him. He's like the best boyfriend in the world! We made out for like an hour and a half today. I went over to his house while his family was gone. It was so hot! I thought that something might've happened, but he didn't try anything and I was okay with running my hand over his back. It felt so good to feel his skin on mine. He said that he wants to take things slow, but I don't know if he really does. I keep feeling him getting excited and it gets me excited. I have to tell you about this because I lied to him. When he asked if I wanted to cool off, I told him, "yes."

# 25

I'm burning my time clone clothes right now. It feels good to get rid of that. I don't know what I would've said if anyone saw them. There was the chance they might've picked up the two sweaters to compare them and if they touched it would've been really bad. With all of the Rainbow Warriors retired, I don't know who would've come to fix the paradox. Maybe Sasha still has her wand so they would've had to summon her away from her paradise. I hope she's happy.

# 26

**February 20**

Brandon came to talk to me last night when I was burning the time clone clothes. I was going to write a lot more. Sorry. I guess he lives on the other side of some trees from The Gate. He said The Gate looked cool. He told me about when he was little he used to pretend it was a gateway into another world. I asked what he would do if it was and he said that he'd probably fall down a hill and break his leg. It was funny. I wish I could take people through The Gate. The Magicals are so nice. I feel like even Mom would have a good time at court.

Mom and Dad were acting shady this morning. Someone from the police station or something wants to talk to me. They wanted to know if I'd feel safer talking to them at home, but I really don't care. The cops got nothing on me. They're never going to find my diary and now that there aren't any time clones, I'll be fine.

## 27

Today is the Sunday that I met Detective Slauson, the closest thing to a super villain since Wikella. He's got the wand and the key, Diary. I don't know what to do.

I should back up. You told me before that it helps to tell events sequentially whenever possible.

So Mom and Dad took me to IHOP and then we went down to the courthouse again. It's like the fifth or sixth time I've been there in the last month, so I wasn't even worried. I met with this nice lady detective. I think her name is Officer Fieldman. She took a lot of my statements when I was first brought in for processing. She asked a lot of non-leading question about sexual assault and I just told her that I wasn't kidnapped or raped. She has the cutest dog in the world, a really big fluffy dog. I think it's a spitz or something. I keep forgetting the breed.

Officer Fieldman brought me into this room with couches and tables that kind of looked like a therapy or council room. The wand and key were sitting on the table!

My eyes went right to them. I almost ran over and stuffed them in my pockets, but I stopped myself. I was in the courthouse. There was probably a camera on me. I tried to act really casual, picking them up and examining them like I'd never seen them before. I even fingered the transformation button on the wand like I was trying to press it but nothing was happening. Eventually I sat down to wait. There was a Shakespeare book in the shelf so I took it out and read Othello; like super caszh!

Detective Slauson came in before I finished the first page. He's built like a football player but he's got eyes like a scientist. Everything he did, he did with purpose. He pulled out the chair at the desk with one foot and sat down in a way that wasn't wasteful but it was different. Slauson didn't start talking right away either, he waited for me to look up from Shakespeare and close it.

I thought he was going to make small talk, so I got ahead of it by talking about the weather and asking him what he'd had for breakfast.

"What does the key open?"

I made some kind of reaction, Diary! I think I flinched! I don't think it mattered what I said after that. I said something like, "which key?"

He picked up the key and showed it. That key looked like a toy in his hands. This guy could put his whole palm on Dad's face. He reminded me of Wikella's ogres. I fought them all the time transformed, but I couldn't have transformed without breaking the Oath!

"Ummm...I don't know. Maybe a kid's toy box or something?"

"These aren't yours?"

I did my best apathetic teenager impersonation, which was pretty good because I happen to be one of those. He didn't buy it. He saw right through me. Slauson kept holding the key out to me like it was a picture of my murder victim and I was losing my cool. I felt the sweat build up on my forehead. He had to have known that I was lying.

"If you want me to have them, I'll take them." I reached for the key and he closed his hand fast as a bear trap.

"I didn't say anything about the other." He pocketed the key and picked up the wand. "It's a strange thing, but definitely not a toy. This is a real emerald on the tip and there's no wiring inside. I took it to the boys down in forensics, asked them to open it up, you know what they told me?"

"We don't get paid to play with toys?"

The joke had the opposite effect on Slauson, he made a smirk but it wasn't a smirk to acknowledge the joke. He smirked to tell me that he was on to me. Slauson turned the wand around in his fingers like he was playing with a darn pencil!

"They said they couldn't open it. I watched them take a reciprocating saw to the hilt. You know what that is?"

I shrugged. "Something that cuts."

He smiled that knowing smile again. It made me so mad to sit there and watch him mock me like that. "Yeah, it's something that cuts. It dulled the blade. They talked about trying to open it with a water jet or sending a microscopic camera into the button, but I knew it was a waste of time."

He waited for me to ask something like, "why's that," but at that point I just kept my eyes on the floor.

Slauson made this gross smacking noise with his lips and teeth and then I heard him sucking. He put the wand in his fudge tasting lips! He was chewing on the thing! I couldn't take it. My hands were balled into fists. My teeth were clenched. I wanted to dust him!

"It tastes like a pixie stick."

I didn't know if it did. I'd never put it in my mouth like an ape on steroids! It's such a weird detail for the Magicals to implement in the design of the wand. They never even told me about it.

Slauson held the wand out to me. "You want to try?"

"That was just in your mouth!"

He shrugged. "I can have someone clean it off. Should I call someone in to clean it, or do you want to tell me how the magic works?"

I cracked again. He's an adult. He can't know about magic. Their minds can't even comprehend the possibility of the fantastic existing, but not Slauson. Something about this mountain of a man still believed in the immaterial. Maybe he read a lot of comics or still collected Science Fiction books from his childhood, but the man believed in the impossible enough to put together the clues and ask me about the nature of magic.

I didn't know adults like that existed, Diary! I didn't know they could exist! Why didn't the Royals tell me about that? Why didn't they warn me that grown ups could believe in magic? If they could, why have I kept all of this a secret from my parents? King Walrus told us that it was because it would break their minds, but Detective Slauson isn't broken. What haven't they told me, Diary?! Why would they keep something like this from me?!

Anyway, I kind of snapped. I started rambling about how there is no magic. I talked about how magic didn't exist and that he was just a bully with a badge. I went on for like twenty minutes about how magic isn't real, how I died, and how he didn't know what he was talking about.

Finally, he asked me, "what am I talking about? If it isn't magic, what is it?"

I shut my mouth far too late. He tried to get me to talk again, but I didn't. He stood up and said that if I wanted them back all I had to do was tell him the truth. He left a business card on the table and left the door open as he left. Another minute later Officer Fieldman came by to escort me back to my parents.

Diary, you have to talk to the Royals. I don't care who you talk to. You can send Princess Platypus for all I care! I need some help getting the wand and key back!

# 28

**February 21**

It was my first day back to school today, Diary. So much happened, but at the same time I'm not even sure what to tell you. I didn't have to lie for the most part. With all of my changes, and with everything that's going on in my life, I didn't even really care about high school. It's just high school. I'm two years from graduation. In five years will I even care about what happened? I have homework right now. How am I supposed to care about homework when I have to figure out how to get the wand and key back from Detective Slauson?

I used to care what other people thought about me at school. I didn't want anyone to notice me because then they'd figure out that I was special. But what's so bad about being special? The other kids noticed me. They were nice to me. So many people told me that they missed me. Lily's friends acted like they were my best friends. They had presents for me. I must've got five dozen roses today. There's this cool swatch for metallic eye shadows that Karekare gave me. I think I'm gonna try out a copper tone tomorrow.

Lily was like...I don't know. She was being her normal self nowadays. Kind of mopey. At least at school she puts on a fake smile. She kept on looking at me like she was being judgy or something so I just stopped looking at her. People are happy to see me. She can either be jealous or she can be my friend because I'm tired of her trying to do both.

Speaking of trying to be friends, the queen bee herself talked to me. I almost told her to take a long walk into a deep lake but Fifi had this look like a dog brought back from the vet. She took forever to say what she wanted to say, but it started with an apology.

She was going on like, "I was never trying to hurt you, Holly. We ran in different circles; that's it. I'm sorry that you felt like no one understood what you were going through, especially if you got that feeling from me. My home life is a mess right now. I feel like when I'm at school, it's the only time that I can be myself. I'm just trying to be happy and sometimes that means I don't pay attention to other people; that I don't see how much pain they're in.

"And I..."

I think she saw how little I cared about her reasons for being selfish, so she kind of trailed off. I heard her sigh.

"I'm sorry, Holly. I just wanted to tell you that. I was hoping that we could try to be friends." She gave another sigh. "I'm...um...not going to get in the way of you and Jaden. I didn't know what was going on with the two of you, I swear. I liked him for probably all of the same reasons that you did and he just..."

The b smiled at me like we had some secret code. She's my enemy. Why doesn't she get that?

"Well, we started to date after you..." She swallowed hard and played with hair.

Like; what? Was she trying to look pretty or something? There weren't any boys around to buy her used tampons. She's just like that; always trying to look like an actress from the CW. Is she just so used to flirting that she can't turn it off? Cause even if I was into girls I could do way better than a skank hoe thot.

"We started going out. Neither of us wanted something to happen, but he was in so much pain and I just...I wanted to see him smile again. I wanted him to be happy."

I think she remembered who she was talking to and stopped herself again. She probably should've stopped talking entirely. It's certainly what I wanted.

"Like I said, Holly. I never wanted to hurt you. After you came back I think Jaden realized what a mistake he'd made. He broke up with me the day after he found out about your return. Think whatever you want about me but..."

She started to cry. It was weird, Diary. I'd fantasized about her crying, but I always wanted her to cry because she was humiliated. Those tears were different. She looked me right in the eyes so I would know how serious she was about this. I think she wanted to take my hands, so I took a step back.

"Please don't blame Jaden for what happened between us. I...I'm not going to get in your way. I just want him to be happy, okay?"

I was mad dogging her when I told Fifi, "he will be."

She half rolled her eyes and then remembered that she was faking being nice and put that wet smile back on. "Okay. Good. I'm glad you're back, Holly. I really am."

What was I going to say to that, thank you? Fifi walked off. I probably shouldn't have said anything, but I needed her to know that I knew what she was doing was an act.

She was almost around the corner when I asked her, "why are you acting so sad?"

"What?" It choked out of her.

"Nobody's going to give you a golden globe. You were with Jad for what, a month, if even? Everyone knows you're just going to find another guy and move on, so you can save the waterworks for someone else."

The facade dropped and the skank scowled at me. "I told you I wasn't here to start a fight. I apologized to you. That isn't enough? What the [f-word] do you want from me?" This hoe growled like a dog with a chicken bone. "Do you want to humiliate me? It's not enough to take my boyfriend, you want to take my friends too?!"

I laughed. "He wasn't your boyfriend. He was never going to be your boyfriend! The only reason he kissed you was because he thought I was dead. So just go find another cute boy to sink your tentacles around, because Jaden and I are in love!"

I don't know how this happened, but Lily was there. She got close to Fifi, maybe to drag her back because the skank looked like she wanted to throw down.

"I'm not a [f-word] slut! I loved him, Holly! I gave my

virginity to him and the second you came back, he dumped me! How the [f-word] do you think that makes me feel?"

"Probably like the slut you are."

Lily's hands were on her shoulders. I think Lily thought the dog was going to come at me, but some psycho stuff started happening. It was like she was the Wicked Witch of the West and somebody threw a bucket of water on her. Fifi's fudging face melted. It sucked in like a grape in the sun. Her entire body constricted. Her little princess nails curled into fists, her knees bent and she slid down to the floor.

I was in no mood for all that drama. "Come on, Lils."

Lily hesitated, probably to give the skank a tissue or something. Fifi's friends were nearby. They were all glowering at me. Like I'd even want friends like that? No, thanks. Fifi can keep her dress-code-breaking, football-player-sucking friends.

Lily hadn't heard all of it. She just wanted to be close by in case Fifi gave up on trying to be civil. Which, all things considered, is probably a good thing. I filled Lily in on her fake apology and all of her attempts to try and take the moral high ground. The whole school knew she was a slut, so I don't know who she thought she was fooling.

Of course, that's probably why Jad dated her when I poofed. I put that together pretty fast after he started getting aroused while we were making out. I get it, he's a guy. I just really thought that he wasn't that kind of guy before. Am I the only teenager in the world who still thinks that sex is a big deal?

I disappear and Jad and Lily both go out and have sex with someone that they knew was bad for them. That bad part of my brain tries to tell me that it has something to do with me disappearing, but I know that's just selfish thinking. Even back in my world, Jad was flirting with Fifi and Lily was talking about how hot her violin teacher was. They were considering have sex with someone that was easy. Jad went for the school slut and Lily went for an older guy because she didn't want to deal with a five second high schooler.

I know that they're my best friend and my boyfriend, but

I kind of feel let down. I really thought that sex was a bigger deal than that to them. I thought that we had that in common. Yeah, when I'm making out with Jad I feel that...heat, but we still haven't done anything. I felt him against me, but that's it. I knew when to stop. I thought Jad would've been able to do that. Maybe that's why he's waiting with me, because he knows I'm not a slut who wants something to happen the moments our lips touch.

It's Lily that really let me down.

No. It isn't Lily's fault. This is just like what happened with Wikella and her puppers. They didn't know what they were doing was wrong. She took away that part of their brain. When I drank whiskey, I didn't think anything of it. I wanted to try it, so I did. Lily isn't the villain here, and neither is Jad. I broke Jad's heart when I took off and that bitter fudge eating dog took his virginity. He was basically raped, they both were.

I wish Jad wasn't busy with homework. I really wanted to see him after all that drama with Fifi.

# 29

**February 22**

Brandon gave me a usb with a bunch of songs he likes. I know that it's supposed to be a big deal, but is it? If he likes me, I should probably let him know that nothing is going to happen. I still haven't told him about Jad, but I also haven't told him about Lily, or me being the Lazarus Girl. I'm not keeping my boyfriend a secret from him because I'm trying to date two guys, I just want one part of my life to be drama free. It's definitely not going to be that way with Lily and Jad.

Fudge! I'm actually going to be late to school.

## 30

So, I got invited to a party. It's this Friday and there's one hundred percent going to be "booze and bongs."

Tiff Tay invited me. I don't think I've ever talked about her because she's a friend of Lily's friend Amber. She's one of those girls that I've known for like my entire life, but we've never had a conversation before. I think she's a JV soccer player. From the sound of things it's mostly going to be her and the other girls in soccer, but she said I could bring Jad because most of them already have boyfriends.

I guess the whole school knows about how I told Fifi, "nobody's gonna give you a golden globe," and so now I'm popular? I keep hearing people say "golden globe" behind my back. I can't help but smile. They all know how fake Fifi is now. She didn't even come to school today. Good.

But yeah, Tiff Tay came up and wanted to know if I'd be down to chill at her place this Friday. She said it was like an after the game thing, but I didn't have to go to the soccer game. I might go to the game anyway because they'll probably be talking about who kicked what when. I haven't cared about sports since before the Magicals recruited us. It might be fun to get back into that.

Tiff Tay kind of talked to me about my swearing. She was like, "so you don't swear but you call people sluts?"

I told her, "there's nothing wrong with telling the truth. No one's going to get mad if I point at a sparrow and call it a bird."

Tiff Tay liked that. I wish I could post memes here sometimes. She laughed a lot when I was talking. It felt good, like how it used to feel when I talked to Lily. If she wants to spend all her time talking trash on the push-up bra patrol, I'm fine with that.

She asked if I would be cool going to a party with booze

and bongs and I told her, "as long as I don't have to do anything."

"For sure! Most of my [b-word] don't smoke. It's just a few of us going outside. Real chill."

So I think I'm going to go.

I told Jad that I wanted to talk to him, but I didn't tell him about the party yet. He said he had a lot of homework today because he's got a big test on Friday and a project due on Monday. I feel like he had zero homework until I went back to school. Oh, and get this! I heard a rumor that I'm getting a passing grade no matter what. Like because I died no one wants to give me an F. I don't know if that's true, but my teachers haven't called on me once.

# 31

That was Jad. We talked for like an hour. He said that he couldn't come over, but I'm only 20 minutes away. I said that I could come to his place, but he doesn't want me walking alone at night. How funny is that! If anyone tried anything, I'd...

Right, no wand. Ugh! I really need that wand.

See, I'm down in the dumps again because I was talking to Jad.

Guess why he's mad at me?

Yep, it's Fifi. Surprise, surprise! She still manages to make my life worse even when I've "won."

After Fifi had her little chat with me, she went crying to Jad about it. Apparently, she only talked to me because Jad told her to!

First of all, it's super sus that he was talking to her in the first place. They're exes. Why would he want to go back to that? Second, why did he think I'd want to talk to her. According to Jad, Fifi should've talked to me because "I thought you'd want to hear it from her." The only thing I wanted to hear from her was, "bye."

I wish that was the only thing we talked about, but he's getting on my case for being "unempathetic." The whole school hearing about me burning Fifi meant that Jad heard about it too. He thinks that I should've just listened to her fake apology and gave her a hug or some mess.

And also I totally called how she was being fake about wanting to apologize! She totally did it just to get on Jad's good side. That bitter bitter bitter cookie! What a pollen hungry bee! She's using Jad again. She's trying to make me out to be the villain by pulling this crying act. Maybe I SHOULD give her a golden globe.

If that's her plan then I need to outplay her. I need to be super super nice to her and make some huge apology. I need to talk to Lily about this. I wish she wasn't being so sketchy lately.

I just texted Lils like, "wyd," and she was just like "hw." I can't remember the last time she tried that excuse. If it wasn't so late, I'd walk over to her house.

# 32

Parents wigged out about me going outside in the middle of the night. Okay, so they gave me a can of mace and a rape whistle. I think that's literally the closest thing to a sex talk we've ever had. Cool. And if that wasn't weird enough they want to sell the rights to my life. There might be a movie about me. Should I turn them down, Diary? Do you even care? Why can't you just send someone through the gate?! That way I wouldn't need to carry around a rape whistle.

# 33

**February 23**

I'm gonna ditch Brandon to have breakfast with Lily. Just telling you in case you pick today of all days to send someone to bring me back to the Magicals. I'm still gonna be there tonight. If not, I'll try to let you know.

# 34

I'm so tired and cold, but if I don't update you, I know you're not going to let me sleep. I'm getting some hot cocoa.

Told Mom I was working on homework. I've done like one assignment since coming back. My teachers don't even care. I should've gone to a world where I killed myself years ago.

Lily wanted to know if I thought she was a slut. I told her that she wasn't. I told her that she was a victim. Telling her about Wikella was obvi bad, so I compared her to a dog and that went super. I mean, she got what I was saying, but she kept bringing it up well after the fact. For some reason, she wants me to be mad at her. She kept saying, "I'm not a victim. I wasn't raped. If anything I raped him."

Like a sixteen-year-old girl can force themselves on a horny twenty-two-year-old. Lily doesn't understand that she only has the idea in her head to come after him because of that guy. He's probably been "correcting her form" by touching her. This guy's in college and he's not able to tell a high schooler "no?" Come on! Lily has Stockholm Syndrome or something because she gets mad every single time I'm putting the blame on the prince of darkness.

At some point Lily was just like, "let's talk about something else."

Cool with me. I told her about Brandon. She went right to the "do you like him?" It was kind of nice having her give me a hard time about "flirting" with other guys. It's me. I don't know how to flirt with a male prostitute. All I do is talk to him. I told her about how he was showing me all this different music. She said she likes My Chemical Romance okay, but they didn't work for me. When I told her I was kind of getting into 30 Seconds to Mars, she called me Joker Kisser. I kept thinking about kissing that cry baby from the newer one, so I'd pretend to gag.

School was whatever. I made another mistake, Diary. My math teacher talked to me after class. I did a problem on a test that I learned during my death. He just said that he was glad I was catching up on the reading, but I didn't. I forgot what I was supposed to know. It's easy to catch the big things, but every day in class feels like every other day. I don't know what I'm supposed to know. If I don't catch up on my reading and my homework, my two week gap is going to be more sus then it needs to. I know that no one probably cares, but paradoxes can still happen.

I hung out with Tiff Tay for the first half of lunch. Her friends are so funny! They swear all the time, but they're good people. I probably lied about something when I was with them, but it's getting harder to remember every little lie. Most of it was little stuff like when I joked about something.

The Future Authors Club met today. Lily caught up with me and wanted to know why I didn't go. Honestly, I'd just forgotten about it. Jad hadn't brought it up last night. He was too busy defending Fifi. Oh, there's something else about Fifi, but I wanna tell you later.

I talked to Lily about my plan to apologize to Fifi. She thought that it might work, but she said that I shouldn't because "apologies should come from the heart."

"Yeah, but she wasn't even apologizing!"

Lily gave me this sour look.

"What?"

"I was there, Holly. She was bawling her eyes out. You broke her."

I rolled my eyes. "I didn't. She's lying. The whole thing was just an act!"

Lily gave a sigh like she didn't know how to deal with me. "Fine. Let's say that you're right. Let's say that Fifi was faking her apology and her tears and all of it. Do you really want to be like her, and start faking apologies to get on Jad's good side."

I didn't and I don't. It was good that I talked to her because it kind of pulled me back a little from all of that dog's head games. "No. I don't. I love Jad. I don't want to lie to him."

Lily was going to leave me but I followed her. I even left my work behind. I needed her to know that I wasn't a bad person.

"I'm not saying you're a different person, Holls. I know that it's you. But you've changed. I don't know what happened to you in hell, but it's changed you."

"You really think I went to hell?"

"Where else did you go?" She swore. "I don't know, Holly. I don't know what's real anymore. We buried you. I saw your body lowered into a [f-word] casket!"

People were watching us. She wiped away a tear, but when I tried to comfort her she just pulled away and walked off. That was the last time we talked today, Diary. I think that she's actually mad at me, but I don't know why. I don't think it has anything to do with Fifi or me lying or with her violin teacher. I hurt her, Diary. I really hurt her and for some reason that isn't eating me up. Have I just become empty inside?

I don't know.

I'm really glad Jad came over tonight.

He hugged me as soon as he saw me. We held each other for like three minutes before he apologized. I felt bad too. I apologized to him about everything with Fifi. He was right. You probably knew that all along. Didn't you, Diary? King Walrus always told us, "It's easy to be a friend to a good person, but it takes true patience and kindness to be kind to those who've only known pain." I forgot that.

I've been forgetting a lot of the things the Magicals have told me. I realized on the walk over to The Gate that I couldn't even remember Bard Cockatoo's voice. Is this part of the magic, Diary? Am I losing my connection to you and the Magicals? Can you even hear me anymore, Diary? Am I forgetting this because I don't want to remember or is it because I've been exiled? I didn't break the Oath. I haven't sworn! I swear in my mind, but Judge Cobra always said that no crimes exist in the mind. Has that changed?

I guess if I don't write about my lies I'll be able to know

for sure. I need to keep writing you. I need to keep coming to the gate. I need to get the wand and key back. I know that. I just don't know how to do that without breaking the Oath. I'm really tempted to tell Jad about everything.

Jad was so sweet tonight. He wrapped us up in a blanket and held me close and kissed the tears off my cheek. Tonight he told me that he still loved Fifi and that somehow made me feel better about the two of them. It would be one thing if he just missed me and had sex with her, but it wasn't like that. He really loved her, but I guess he loves me too. Jad says that he doesn't want to go back to her though. He says that he's happier now that I'm back. I need to trust him that he wants to stay with me. Besides, there might not be any competition.

Fifi was at school today, but she came by with her parents. They're taking her out of the school. She's gonna have a fresh start over by Greenwood. I hope things are better for her there. I feel bad about how I treated her, but thinking back on how I felt, I don't think she wants to hear me apologize.

I talked to Jad about the party on Friday and he doesn't think that we should go. He's nervous about being the only nerd there, which is kind of cute. He's not a nerd, like not at all. He's really handsome and kind besides. I don't want to be with a jock. I think he knows that but he's nervous about the party.

But the real reason he doesn't want us to go is because he wants me to meet his parents! Like go to his house and meet his parents in a formal dinner. I know I'm going to mess things up. Maybe I can get a fancy outfit or something. How am I supposed to dress when I'm meeting my boyfriend's parents?

I think Jad wants to meet my parents too, but I barely even talk about them. I think he knows that I don't really want to spend a lot of time with them. I mean, don't get me wrong, they've been cooler since I came to World B, but they're still Mom and Dad. I'm honestly surprised they didn't get divorced the day after I killed myself. I guess the mourning was bigger than their misery. They do love me, they've just been terrible at showing it to me.

Oh and Lily ruined 30 Seconds to Mars. I keep seeing that shirtless Joker squirming around when I listen to them.

# 35

**February 24**

Met Brandon this morning. He was there yesterday. He said he made a pyramid of stones in my place. We traded numbers. I think he'd been wanting to do it for a while. Not like Brandon flipped when he got it. We didn't really talk about music today. I think he could see that I was feeling bad.

I've been wondering if the meds I'm on are frying my brain. It felt good at first, but when I think about the past couple weeks, or even the past few days, my brain is all over the place. I don't feel like me, which is kind of the point, right? I came here to get away from my life, to get away from me and my old friend, misery. It's not gone, not really, but there's this like haze around me. When things get bad I'm not consumed by that scratch on my heart, but shouldn't I be? Is how I'm reacting now normal or are these drugs hardwiring my brain?

Brandon said that stopping cold turkey might not even be helpful because I'd be expecting to feel bad or to feel things bigly like before. Bigly was my word for how it was before. Brandon thinks that people talk themselves into being in a mood. Like if I'm going to the store to buy cake, I put myself in a good mood and I might focus on a cute boy or a cool song on the way, but if I'm going there to buy tampons I'm already not having it.

He talked about this thing called "Listening to Gaia." The idea is to experience life without expectations and only react to what's there and not what you're feeling. He's been training himself to do this by listening to music and sitting. Sometimes when he turns the music off, he says that he can hear the heartbeat of Gaia, that he can feel her breathing.

When I told Jad about this, he said, "isn't that just

meditating?"

Okay, but is it? I've never meditated myself, but that doesn't sound like what meditation is. Isn't meditation just sitting there and breathing? It's supposed to be calming, but I don't think you're supposed to listen so much as you're supposed to close your ears.

I really want to call Brandon and talk about this stuff, but it's like nine o'clock. I can just talk to him in the morning anyway.

Today was pretty chill. I think talking to Brandon helped. Yeah, that's what therapy's supposed to be like, but it's always the opposite for me. It doesn't matter if it's this therapist that Bolly had or the school counselor. They want to fix me. That's why they're there, because I'm "damaged" and they're here to fix me. Except they don't fix anything. They just make me think about how I think and offer advice that probably wasn't even helpful when they were kids. I feel like between you, them, and Jad, I have like four people listening to every little thing I do.

Not that I resent you or Jad. Sometimes I just want to exist.

Tiff was totally cool about me not going to her house on Friday. I offered to go watch her play and she went, "why?" Her face had me rolling! I'm going to go anyway, especially since it sounds like no one ever goes to watch their games. I told her that I was going to meet Jad's parents on Friday and she offered to pray for me!

Tiff and her friends told me all these stories about how meeting the parents is usually a sign that you're going to have your first really big fight. It sounds like most relationships don't survive a fight. They told me all these stories about how guys would just drop bombshells like, "our daughter's going to be named, Melody," or talk about how he doesn't like her friends. I think Jad and I already had our big fight though, when we were talking about Fifi. Tiff says she doesn't even bother with meeting parents anymore. She was like, "as long as I'm still getting my period I don't need to know his dog's name." She's so funny!

I guess when a guy invites you to his house it means that

he wants to bone there, but he doesn't want his parents to flip when they come back from the store or whatever. I mean, if I had to choose between his house and mine I'd probably want to be at Jad's. We talked about sex last night and a little today. We both want to. I want to and I've decided that I'm not going to apologize about that anymore. Diary, if you don't want to hear about my love life or my sex life, you can just send someone through The Gate to tell me otherwise. I'm going to lose my virginity to Jad. I've made up my mind. It's just a matter of it being the right time and I guess the right place.

## 36

**February 25**


Lily wants us to walk to school again today, so I'm not going to be at the gate. I should text Brandon so he's not out there waiting for me. Oh, I didn't tell you. Brandon is homeschooled so that's why he can just wait at the gate with me and talk for like two hours. Our conversations have been shorter after starting school.

# 37

I talked to Brandon about Listening to Gaia and meditation. He says that they're different but the same like glass and ice. I told him that didn't make sense and he was like, "it does if you don't think about it." Sometimes I don't know if he's the smartest person I know or the dumbest.

# 38

Mom got me this adorable outfit for my meeting with Jad's parents. It's black with these deep navy blue ribbons in them. It looks classy but fun. She said that when she saw it she thought of me. Thanks, Mom. I look older in it, like I could be a college freshman. I was just going to do natural makeup, but I wanted to do blue lip liner, so I just colored my lips. It matches the dress suit though, which I think works. I wish I could just send you a picture, Diary. I'm so nervous about tonight. If Jad's parents don't like me am I going to have to sneak around?

I better tell you about the game and the drive home now, because something tells me I'm going to have to lie a lot tonight!

First of all, the best part about going to Tiff's game was waiting around for it to start. I met up with Jad outside Yearbook, just like in the old days. Except this time we went around the comp lab to make out a little. It was really fun. He kept telling me how pretty I was and how much he loved me and he was like 100% handsome today! I kept kissing him on the neck and I think I might've given him a hickey. I don't know. I hope I didn't because that would be really bad timing. I told him sorry, but I wasn't. The way he was moaning was like pure caramel.

After that I met up with Lily and her friends. I guess they don't usually go to the game, but they did because I was going. Is it bad that hearing that made me feel like I was flying? I already felt good because of my time with Jad. I think they all knew I was with him before because they all asked how Jad was doing. It's kind of fun to be teased about having a boyfriend.

It got a little awkward because we were talking about kissing and some of the things we liked. Lily had to stay quiet because her friends don't know about her violin teacher. Maybe they do, because she kind of gave me this look like she was trying to figure out if she should tell them or not. I just looked away. That's not on me. I think from the way she looked at me that things are still happening with him. I wish I knew what to do about violin teacher.

Lily won't listen to me about him. I don't know if it's because I'm a virgin or because I keep calling him what he is, a statutory rapist. People like to lie. It's no wonder I have to tell you about almost every conversation I have.

I got to talk to Lily for a few minutes without everyone else around. She asked me how things really were with Jad and I told her about how we were planning to have sex when it felt right. She got this weird look in her eyes. I think it was jealousy. I asked her about it and she just said, "you wouldn't want to hear it." What the fudge covered brownie is that?! I'm only her best friend, why wouldn't I want to talk to her?

Tiff was amazing! She said that she was the team's forward, I didn't realize that she made most of the goals. Tiff was a superstar. Every time the other team had the ball she was running and shouting. I could hear her over the crowd! Tiff isn't that much taller than me but I think it's all in her legs because she flew across the field. I was really into it but Lily and her friends didn't care.

Amber was like, "all that matters is them winning."

"Why?"

"If they lose, the afterparties are super awkward. The team keeps fighting."

Well, she said that but with more cursing.

Tiff really wanted me to come, even if it was just for thirty minutes. I told her about how I had to change and she said I could change at her place. It was funny but really nice. There's something about how Tiff talks that always cracks me up. She just loves life, you know? Like Jad is cool, but he's really serious and he's always thinking about other people's feelings. Brandon is serious in the other way, like he forgets Earth has people on it. Lily used to be fun, but she's such a drama queen lately. I ended up telling Tiff that.

Oh, I went to Tiff's house, that's when I talked to her about Lily. I was trying to tell her that I couldn't go, but then she offered to drive me home and I couldn't really say "no." Tiff drives her mom's old minivan. It isn't fast or cool but it's a lot of fun inside because she can fit like half the team.

Okay, but something weird happened, and I don't know what it means or if it means anything at all!

Mom's calling, I gotta go to Jad's. Wish me luck!

# 39

I had a little fight with Dad when I tried to leave tonight. They didn't want me to go to The Gate because it was so late and it was raining. It's not even raining. It's barely drizzling but Dad has to make a big deal out of everything. Good to know he's back to his controlling ways already. I'm staying behind, but only because I'm so tired. Please don't make this the one time that you actually send someone through the gate.

Mom and Dad wanted to know why it was so important that I go outside every morning and night. They thought I was going to see Jad, so they kind of knew that I was doing something different since Jad and his parents dropped me off. I just told them, "I like to walk. It makes me feel better." They dropped it after that, but they were acting weird again. Dad said that he wants to meet Jad. He's already met Jad, so I don't know what he really wants.

Do you want to know about dinner with Jad's parents or what happened at Tiff's house? Diary, I know you like to hear about what's happening in order, but I don't always want to talk about things in order. This is supposed to be for me, right? I write about lies so they're not so heavy. I admit my feelings so they aren't so bigly.

Jad's mom was weird. She's one of those people that smiles all the time, but she's never happy. Jad's dad seemed nicer, but he was distracted. He kept "checking emails" at the dinner table. He'd be talking about something his students would say and then there'd be a ding and he'd just stop everything and put his nose into his phone. I had to call him Dr. Mills, how weird is that? But like, when I called Jad's mom Mrs. Mills, she insisted that I call her Jennifer.

I know I told you that Jad's dad is a professor, but I didn't know he taught computer science. One of the reasons he's always checking his phone is because he's in charge of this super computer down at the university. He says that students are always running different experiments and messing up the network, but I think he's having an affair.

When Mom was having an affair, all of her excuses sounded perfectly reasonable, but when she actually had to work late when I was younger, she'd barely talked about it at all. Sometimes she'd be grumbling and halfway through the door before she'd remember to tell Dad or me where she was going. I mean, I obvi dunno, but it's sus.

I spent most of the time just whispering to Jad whenever they weren't paying attention to us. We were watching TV "with his dad" so I couldn't hear everything. We mostly just talked about how we were nervous. It was a lot of Jad assuring me that his parents were always like this.

You wanna know the worst part about dinner at Jad's? No one even commented on my outfit. Jad leaned in and said I looked hot, but his parents didn't seem to care. His mom went through the motion of cooking and she didn't talk to me when I was helping her clean the dishes. She even stopped cleaning and poured herself a glass of wine.

After dinner I went to Jad's room. He closed the door and I got nervous. "Don't we have to open the door?"

"Huh? No, they don't care. Whenever Mom drinks, she just goes into her room and locks the door. Dad's probably gonna be in the study until he's too tired to do anything."

"Does she drink a lot?"

"My mom?" Jad got a little closed off, like his posture pulled into himself. "Sometimes. It doesn't get that bad though. It's nothing like how she was on Gabapentin."

He said it like I should know what he was talking about, but he'd never talked about his mom's drug habits. He saw my confusion and said, "the sleep pills."

Diary, I wish you could tell me if I mentioned it before. I feel really bad if I forgot about him telling me that his mom was abusing sleep pills. I kept looking at him, hoping that he'd remember that he told Fifi about his mom instead, but he just took off his shoes. I think he told Bolly about it, but that doesn't make any sense. Bolly is supposed to be just like me except all of the Magicals are a make believe world she and the Rainbow Warriors played in. Why would that mean that Jad would tell her about his mom's drug problems but not me? Was Bolly closer to him than I was to my Jad?

Jad put his arm over my back. "You good?"

I wasn't, but I nodded. "Is it cool if I don't want to make out?"

"Yeah. I mean, you look hot, but this was a lot. I know how weird my 'rents are."

"They're mostly human."

Jad chuckled. "That's an accurate way to describe them."

I ran a hand through his hair. "You look hot too."

"Like a coal?"

"Mmm. Like a bonfire."

"If I knew you liked a button up shirt so much, I'd wear them at school."

"What about on a date?"

"Oh." Jad blushed. "I haven't taken you on one of those, huh?"

I laughed. "No, you haven't. I thought we'd be going to movies and talking over two sprigs of broccoli that cost a hundred dollars."

"I don't know how to tell you this, but I don't have that kind of money. Most of my allowance goes to meals and..." he gestured about his room. I didn't see anything new that would've soaked up his money. Maybe he was talking about his cologne or something, he smelled different.

I took his hand when I asked him, "we are going to go on dates, right?"

He kissed my cheek. "Of course. I just gotta find the money. I kind of like hanging out with you more. If we're at the movies, it's dark and I can't kiss you."

"You'll have to be a gentleman and content yourself with

staring at my regal countenance."

He laughed like I'd never talked that way before, and that's probably because Bolly hadn't. We kissed a little, but not like we'd done before. He ended up giving me a foot rub. He thanked me a lot for putting up with his parents and getting all dressed up. Jad took my picture a lot. I thought I looked real cute. I'm glad I have his picture too. I'm surprised at how good he is at posing for the camera.

Jad's dad knocked on the door like an hour later. We weren't doing anything, but we both had perfect posture the second we heard the knock. His mom came with him and they both thanked me for coming over. They didn't seem to care about my compliments to them. I hope Jad will tell me what's up with them again in the future.

I couldn't really relax with him tonight. I kept thinking about how he was in love with Bolly and how I'm Holly. She killed herself for a reason. If she was closer to Jad than me, what was she going through?

# 40

I was about to try going to sleep. I can't believe I forgot to tell you about Tiff's house.

When we got to her place, Tiff had me follow her. She went right to her room and started changing. I turned around and closed the door. Tiff just laughed at me.

"I promise I'm not a lesbian, [b-word]. It's no big."

"Sorry. I'm still kind of shy about nudity."

"So you and Jaden haven't sealed the deal, huh?"

I shook my head. "We want to. We're both just kind of waiting for the right time, you know?"

She made this noise. It was kind of like a huh, but I don't think she believed me.

"What?"

"I don't know if I should tell you this because hoes lie."

"If you know something about Jaden, I want to know."

"A'ight. He and Fifi first had sex three days after you died. I don't know if it's true, but I believe it. Whenever I saw them together, Jaden couldn't keep his hands off her."

"You mean at school?"

She was done changing and sat on the bed. "Just wherever. Look, you're probably gonna find out about this at some point, but I didn't just know Jaden from school. Fifi would take him to Allie's parties, so I ended up seeing the two of them together a few times. I don't know what Jaden told you about them, but from what I saw, their relationship was all about sex. Even when they were out in the living room with everyone else, he'd be kissing her, necking her, or trying to start something."

I shrugged. "Fifi's a slut."

"Yeah, but from what I heard, that's not all of it. Allie and Fifi both went to Testament Middle. They used to braid each other's hair and tell each other everything, but they fell out when Allie decided to get serious about being a goalie. Fifi hit up Allie after she and Jaden got serious. She wanted to talk to Allie because Jaden was being really...pushy."

"What do you mean?"

Tiff shrugged. "Maybe this isn't my place to say."

"Tiff, you're talking about my boyfriend. If people are saying things about him, I want to know."

"The way I hear it, Jaden initiated sex their first time. She was really into him and he was in a lot of pain, so she just kind of went with it. She got scared that he was going to use her, but he didn't tell anyone about them and he wrote her these love notes or something, Allie didn't see them, but supposedly Fifi really liked them. They were like Hallmark and Shakspeare [s-word], you know?"

I nodded. "So how was he pushy?"

"They kept having sex. Like every time they'd meet Jaden would want to get down. The way Allie tells it, they didn't have a relationship outside of the bedroom. He was either crying, or putting the moves on her. Fifi started taking him to Allie's parties because she wanted a little distance. She was trying to get him to talk to other people."

"But now that it's just me and Jaden, you're surprised that he's not all over me."

Tiff sighed. "I don't think it's you, or maybe it is. You're attractive, Holly. I'm sure that he's into you, but if Jaden is waiting, I don't think it's because he wants to."

I didn't know what to say to that. I was so overwhelmed by all of this and it's more than a little part of why I didn't want to make out with Jad at his house. When I think back on my conversation with Jad and how he invited me to meet his parents, he said, "I kind of wanted to take you to my place," and then I asked, "you mean to meet your parents?" and he nodded. Like there's the possibility that he just wanted me to come over so we could have sex. I was excited to meet his parents because that meant that he was serious about me, but maybe once he saw my enthusiasm, he couldn't say no.

Tiff got my attention and I kind of snapped at her.

"You're trying to warn me. This whole thing about dragging me to your house, it was just to warn me. Is that why you became friends with me?"

"No." She waved her hands around. "No! I swear. I went out of my way to be friends with you because you're a bad[a-word] [b-word]."

It felt good to know that. "Thanks."

"Are you still going to go to Jaden's tonight?"

"Yeah, I mean he hasn't tried anything. If he was pushy with Fifi, maybe that's just because of Fifi. He's never been like that with me."

"Okay. But if you need anything, call me. You can text too. We always have someone sober here, alright?"

I nodded. It felt good to know that I had a house full of amazon warriors ready to kick a guy in the nuts. It felt better than having a can of mace in my purse. But it felt weird to think that I'd need that protection from Jad. I trust him. I love him. So why can't I shake the thought that Tiff wasn't lying to me?

# 41

**February 26**

I dreamt this morning that I went to see Brandon and he whipped his dick out. He was like trying to show me how people head banged with it. The weirdest part was that I just sat there with a plastic smile on my face. I nodded and went "cool, man." So when I woke, I didn't want to talk to Brandon. I laid in bed with my head on the foot of the bed and stared at the wood grain for probably an hour. Mom checked on me and I told her that I was fine. I got a couple texts, but I didn't want to check them. For some reason, the only thing that got me out of that funk was when Tiff called me; something about the incessant buzz against the wood made me answer.

She was getting a breakfast burrito and talked me into going out with her. I tried to tell her "no," but I didn't try very hard. Tiff got me to chuckle by telling me, "if you're gonna be a mope, it's better to do it with friends." It didn't make any sense, but going out with Tiff felt easy. I put on some of my old clothes and Tiff called me, "Holly classic." It was weird having Tiff refer to my past.

One thing about Tiffany Taylor that I don't think I've mentioned, is that the girl can eat. She ate a breakfast burrito and an entire order of Irish nachos basically by herself. According to Tiff, breakfast burritos are the perfect food for dealing with a hangover. I made a fool of myself in front of her, asking "should you drive with a hangover?" It really cracked her up. She said it was basically just like having a headache.

I think Tiff knew I had a lot going on in my mind, so she kind of just let me eat and chill, but she didn't go on her phone or anything. Even after we were done eating, we sat in the car and listened to the sound of the rain pelting the roof. I love the smell of the wet earth. Some people hate running out in the rain, but I'd be okay if it rained every day. There's something about how the drops collect and make little rivers on the windshield. Those drops got somewhere to go. I almost cried thinking about how I don't. Summer is coming but I still have my white fur.

"Are you a virgin, Tiff?"

"No. Thank [f-word], no."

I didn't know if she wanted to talk about it, so I didn't pressure her, but she was waiting for me to say something more.

Her first time was with this guy she met on summer vacation. She said it helped to know that no matter what, he wasn't going to talk to anyone at school, but he didn't seem like the bragging type. Tiff described him as one of those stoner types, but he was really into dance and he tried to do all of this parkour stuff. They were both kind of shy, so Tiff had to make the first move.

"He'd be dancing and sometimes I would just watch him and bite my lip. I got tired of watching him writhe on the ground and wondering what sex was like, so I was gonna do it. One day we ran out too far and had to take a bus back. I took his hand and told him straight up, 'I wanna [f-word] you.' He..." she laughed thinking back about it. "He was like, 'pretty sure I'm the one who has to do the [f-word].' After that, it was kind of like a challenge. You know, we hooked up, and I focused on what we were doing. At some point, I thought he was going to say he loved me and I told him I'd punch him if he did. The laughing helped. I've heard some girls really hate their first time.

"But, I mean, you and Jaden are going to be different. You still haven't done anything, right?"

"No." I chewed on my straw. If it bothered Tiff, she didn't tell me. "It was awkward last night. He was a gentleman, but I really didn't know how to act. I kept thinking about what you told me."

"What were you worried about?"

"Everything. If he was all over Fifi, then why was he able

to be so patient with me? Was I a bad girlfriend for not putting out right away? Was I overthinking everything? I don't know. I didn't have any answers. Dating Jad isn't how I thought it would be. No dates going out to the movies. We don't spend every lunch together holding hands. I barely see him at school."

Tiff chuckled a bit. "Get used to that bit about guys not taking you out on dates. I don't know if it's just because we're in high school, but the guys I've dated only take me out when we can't stay in, you know? Where have you been meeting?"

"Before last night, we were always meeting outside somewhere. I don't even know if he wanted me to meet his parents. He asked me to go to his house, and I thought he wanted me to meet them."

Tiff was quiet. I played with my straw, poking it in and out like a hundred times before I put it in the cup holder and apologized. She didn't say nothing about it, I just didn't want to be a weirdo. "Y'think I'm weird for not wanting to have sex right away?"

"Nah. Most girls I know do, but it's different when you play sports. I don't know if it's cause we spend so much time thinking about our bodies, or if the girls in soccer are just horny, but everyone in the team doesn't want to wait. Well, except for D-nice, but I don't even know why she's in the team, she does everything different.

"From what I've seen, there are two types of girls, those that listen to their bodies and want to get it, and those that think their first time is gonna be with candles and pop music playing in the background. Well, then there are the push-up hoes but there's a difference between being a slut and wanting the d, you know?"

I didn't.

"It's like..." Tiff thought about how to explain it. "Okay, so before you had a thing for Jaden, you'd check guys out, right?"

I tried to think back. That was so long ago. I ended up telling Tiffany, "Jaden was my first crush. I haven't really liked any other guys."

"No one?"

I shook my head.

"Good for him, I guess. So girls will be like, 'oh he's cute,' or 'that guy has a nice smile, I want to talk to him more,' and maybe they do, maybe they don't. But a slut goes around school waiting for guys to come to her. She doesn't care how she gets it, she just wants it. She wants boys to like her because it makes her popular. But she doesn't care who is after her, as long as they're halfway decent looking.

"Like..." she thought about it. "You know Nells, right?"

"She's in the team. Hair's kind of in a mop."

"Yeah, she wears gloss that's too pink for her face. I love Nells like a sister, but that girl doesn't care who she's with. The second she finds out a girl's willing to date other girls, Nells pounces on them. I literally heard her say, 'gimme that clam.'"

It sounded funny on her lips, so I tried it out. "Gimme that clam."

We giggled about that. Well, I giggled. Tiff doesn't really giggle.

"Anyway, it's not cause Nells is a lesbian either. She and Roxy were together for not even three months. After they broke up, Rox was still hung up on her, but Nells has been with..." She smacked her lips. She did that when she thought sometimes. "Like six other girls since they broke up. Homegirl will drive to other counties to get some, you feel me?"

See what I mean about Tiff being funny? I'm so glad we're friends!

I told Tiff, "Sluts want some all the time no matter what, but everyone else only wants it from the right guy."

"Exactly. If Jad's doing it for you and you want some of that, go for it, but you gotta know that it's what you want. Because I'm telling you right now, there aren't going to be candles. [f-word]! You probably won't even get there unless you reach down and take care of it yourself."

I wasn't expecting to hear that. I must've looked like a tomato, because Tiff started calling me a prude. It wasn't mean, though. I like it when she teases me. I never feel like I have to agree with her, you know?

We'd never talked about that before and I haven't even talked to you about that either. Well, I do it, okay? I masterbate. I've been doing it for awhile now. It doesn't make me a bad person and if I haven't been doing it, I think I would've done something dead brain by now. After making out or sometimes just thinking about Jad, I can't stop thinking about him until I do something about it. Ugh! I hate how I can't talk to you anymore. I have to make all of these guesses about what you're thinking.

First time I did it, I thought Sheriff Bulldog was gonna throw me in the dungeon, but no one even looked at me. I should've known nothing was up when the key still worked, but I'm not always the smartest person. Anyway, I masterbate, and now you know that about me.

I think it helped to talk to Tiffany about this. It made me want to try sex and it made me want to try it with Jad. I thought that I was gonna come home and call up Jad and ask if we could do it today, but every time I was about to hit send, I deleted what I wrote. One of the texts I wrote was just, "dtf?" My finger was literally a milimeter away from hitting send. Can you imagine if I sent him that? He probably would've thought I was a slut then. Maybe he already does. Maybe he wants a slut, I don't know. He was with Fifi, right?

But Fifi wanted something more than sex. Tiff believed that and I believe her. It's too weird for her to make that up, especially since she dragged me to her house to talk to me about it. I think I know what I need to do, but I really don't want to. I need to call Lily.

I know that she hates me. I feel like the second I go over to her place, we're just going to have another fight. But I've known Lily the longest and she knows Jad the best. The two of them were really close last year, maybe even closer than me.

Oh, Brandon texted me. He says that we should meet up for real, like actual friends. What a geek, right? Nah, I'm just playing. I'll probably hang out with him tomorrow.

# 42

Lily finally told me why she's mad at me and I don't know if I can be mad at her for feeling that way.

I kind of broke down and cried with her. We were both crying for almost an hour. At some point it was just us drinking water, blowing our noses, and pissing. I had to tinkle after Lily went right after me, and we both laughed for the first time in what felt like a week. Things have been so tense with us. I'm glad we finally talked about everything.

My hand kind of hurts from writing earlier, but I know you don't care, Diary.

She's mad at me for killing myself. It sounds silly, but it's the truth. When I took my life, I didn't just give up on her, but I gave up on our friendship. Lily told me about how she loves me and how our friendship means so much more to her than text messages and talking at school. When she thinks about her life five, ten, even fifty years from now, she sees me there. She says I didn't, and she's right.

Ever since I was a kid, I always thought that the time would come when I would leave Earth and come to live with the Magicals. I know that any real person who stays there too long can never come back, but that's why I'm here dating Jad. That's why I want to drink and have sex and do everything that Earth has to offer, because I know that once I decide to stay there, that's it. There is no alcohol in the castle. I don't even know if anyone has penises or vaginas. I mean, you're all flat down there. I was going to leave Earth after graduation.

If I went to college, I'd be taken away from the gate. And once I started moving around, there's the chance that I'd lose the key, or worse yet someone would find it. I guess that already happened and after my first move. I couldn't have kept the key on me, I know I couldn't. The police took all my clothes and

I didn't have any time to hide the key. Maybe they would've just thought it was a toy, but not with that assumptive baster Detective Slauson working the force.

That's why I can't break the Oath, Diary. I want to spend most of my life there in the castle with you and the Royals. I want you and Captain Alligator, and everyone to see me grow old. I don't want to turn my back on you the way Sashy and Finn did. You all gave us so much. The three of us are the last of the Rainbow Warriors, and they acted like none of that even mattered. Sashy wanted a normal life and Finn pretended he had one, but I want to be one of the Magicals! Please don't tell the others about this, Diary. I was going to surprise everyone. I still want to. I just need some help getting the key back. Please convince them to send someone.

I'm so thoughtful, but I'm also really tired. It's not even six, but I need to take a nap.

# 43

I found Bolly's diaries. They're all written with secret markers, just like mine. If I run the revealer over them, I'll be able to know what she talked to Jad about, but I'll be breaking her privacy. Do you think it's wrong to do it? I mean, her parents and maybe even the police went through the house after she died and they didn't find these. If I read them, I can know why she killed herself. Maybe I won't find out the whole truth, but I'll at least have a better idea.

I thought of a way to trick Detective Slauson, but it won't work. Any lie I come up with needs to use the button on the wand. It's clearly a button and if I don't use it for something, I won't be able to trick him. I really wish I hadn't sworn to never change in front of the uninformed. Slauson could be a servant of evil, but Wikella is dead. She was the only evil thing, right? The royals would gain nothing by keeping another evil from us.

I can feel my mind working on this problem. I can beat Slauson. I just need to find some way to convince him that I can resurrect the dead.

Jad came over. I forgot that he called when I was out with Lily, so he got worried and came by. Mom and Dad took off a little after, which was sus because they don't usually go out in the middle of the night. Dad was like, "you okay to get food?" and then they took off. They wanted to give me some time alone with Jad. They never would've done that in my world. Do they feel guilty about me taking my life? Have they just been walking on eggshells this whole time? Fudge with nuts, maybe they have.

It was really nice having him here all to myself. He got me a present, but it's a present that doesn't make any sense. He knew about how I wanted to live in the Magical Castle. He had Lily draw a version of King Walrus and Queen Nephila. I was in the picture too, but as a cartoon. Jad got me a plastic gold tiara and a big walrus and spider. It weirded me out. It's not the right kind of spider, but it was a nice gesture for Bolly.

Bolly told them about the Magicals. She told them about everyone except you, Diary. I was too hung up on that to even make out with Jad. Okay, so we made out a little, but it wasn't like really intense. He held me and told me about the war with Wikella, how I fought the Troops of Evil, and even how I became her pupper and drank Dad's whiskey. He knew all of that.

I know that Bolly wasn't a Rainbow Warrior, because she doesn't have the scars, but why would she tell them...

I must have one brain cell. It's so obvious! She never took the Oath, not really. It was just some childhood game to her. There was no reason to keep that secret from Jad or Lily. They're closer because Bolly didn't need to lie to them. Does that mean I can talk to them about what happened to me? I wouldn't be breaking the Oath if they already know I was a Rainbow Warrior, right? I just don't have to tell them that it was real.

Ah! I wish there was some way to confirm this.

I went to Lily's house to talk about Fifi. She convinced me that I need to get Fifi's side of her relationship with Jad. I took her boyfriend and she left the school to get away from me. Going to talk to her would be like talking to Wikella, but I did that. That's how we were finally able to defeat Wikella. All of us at our strongest couldn't get past her defenses, but she let me through to talk because she thought she could corrupt me; and she did. I need something to get past Fifi's defenses. But Fifi isn't a villain, right?

Ugh! I'm so confused! I wish I could just look at her with spectral glasses and know if she's good or not.

Lily thinks that I need to talk to Fifi. Even if I don't ask her about all the sex stuff, she says I need to apologize to her. Maybe I do. I don't want to. I just want to know if she seduced Jad or if he just cares about sex. But he isn't like that with me. Guys that are only looking to get laid don't bring you really personal presents, right?

Jad's taking me on a date tomorrow. If I'm gonna talk to

Fifi before that, I'll need to try to call her tonight.

Diary! Please just let me sleep if I have to lie to Fifi tonight!

# 44

**February 27**

I had to flake on Brandon again today, but I promised to see him Monday. He doesn't want to meet, he wants to go somewhere with me. I told him I could do Monday night. He said his older sister could take us. She's like twenty so he said it wouldn't be weird. Why did that make it sound weirder?!

I have important stuff to do. I don't know why I keep talking to you about Brandon. Jad knows about him, but I still don't feel like I can talk to Jad about him. They're both so different from each other. Brandon thinks about things like stars having souls and what music sounded like in ancient mesopotamia and Jad just isn't interested in any of that. He cares about what's real. You're the only friend that might understand Brandon, Diary.

Tiff talked to Allie who talked to Fifi and she texted last night. She said that she'd have lunch with me, but her brother is going to be there. I guess she thinks I might attack her or something, but I wouldn't. I weigh like ninety pounds, who am I going to hurt even if I did? All of my time as a Rainbow Warrior won't help me in an actual fight.

I hate that I have to apologize to Fifi!

# 45

Tiff was telling the truth. Everything Allie told her about Jad was true. I know what it looks like when people are lying and Fifi wasn't lying. I don't know what this means. I wish I could write this all down and figure it out, but I have my date with Jad.

## 46

I'm at The Gate right now. Please send someone, Diary. Please! I need some real answers! I need to know if I can reveal Bolly's diary!

It's so hard to write under an umbrella.

My date went well. It was really sweet just holding his hand and watching the movie, but I kept wanting to lean over and whisper into Jad's ear. We didn't do anything in the theater, but we made out a little on the bus. I think he gave me a hickey. It's a good thing it's turtle neck weather, and that I bought scarves and turtlenecks last week. I'm a horny woman, Diary. I came to this world to make this happen.

I keep thinking about Fifi. She almost sounded scared of Jad. Hold on, Fifi is texting me right now.

# 47

She thinks Jad cheated on one of us. I told her about what happened and...ah! Okay, my mind is all over the place. Lemme go back to this morning. Actually, I should tell you about last night too.

Fifi texted me, "I'll meet with you to talk about what happened with Jaden, but I don't want to hear an apology from you or I swear to [g-word] I will pull out a chunk of your hair. I don't want to see how you would win a golden globe."

I told her, "okay, can you meet tomorrow morning?"

"Noon at Arcadia. My older brother is going to be there and he has no problems punching a [b-word]."

I guess it makes sense that she was so defensive. I had to text Jad to reschedule, but he was okay about it. I ended up telling him that my mom wanted to take me shopping, which was only a half lie because we bought a couple things at Arcadia.

It took a little while to find Fifi because she was sitting somewhere in the mall that I'd never been to. The rain stopped, but all the outdoor tables were still wet. I had to wipe my hand over the seat to clean it. She had a newspaper that she'd used to wipe hers off and she didn't offer it. I guess she wanted to humiliate me a little. Fine.

I sat on the moist seat because I needed to know what was up with Jad. Her brother was there by the way. She wasn't just making that up. He had glasses on and he was crossing his arms and trying to look tough. I wanted to go, "you're 18 and a buck fifty, I'm not scared of you."

Fifi got right to it, "here's what's going to happen. You're going to sit there and I'm going to tell you how Jad and I started dating and what happened. If I don't still feel like throwing up, I'll listen to how you stole him from me. Then we never have to talk to each other again, fair?"

"Fair as fiction?"

She scowled.

"Yeah, we're good." I waved for her to get to it.

Most of what she said I already knew third hand from Tiff, but their relationship started completely different than I thought. Jad had been flirting with Fifi before I poofed. He'd been flirting with her for almost a month before. The way Fifi tells it, she kind of knew that we were close friends, so she didn't want to get in the way of things.

Jad asked her out and she basically turned him down. She told him, "I like you, but it seems like you have something going on with someone else. Maybe it would be best if we stayed friends."

Jad acted cool about it but like a week later he asked her out again "as friends." Fifi wasn't sure about it, but she told him "yes," thinking that she could just cancel if she felt weird about it later. That's when Fifi really surprised me, because she called Lily. Lily told Fifi that I was completely head over heels for Jad, and that if she and Jad started dating, it would break my heart.

I guess it did.

Fifi canceled but Jad kind of freaked out and he kept texting her, "can I call you?" "we need to talk." Finally, Fifi caved and they talked on the phone. He wanted to know if Fifi was blowing him off, so she just said "yes." Then completely unprompted, he started going on about how he wasn't in love with anyone, how he didn't have feelings for anyone else.

I guess Fifi was looking out for me, and asked if anyone was interested in him and he just said, "So what if they are? I can't control how other people feel about me." She got really upset and told him that she really didn't want to date him and she felt like he was lying to her to try and get her to go on a date anyway.

And he was. Jad admitted it.

Fifi said that he apologized and that she ultimately did forgive him, but she made Jad promise that he wouldn't try to trick her into going out on a date again. Jad told her, "Alright, next time I ask you out, it'll be for real."

And then Fifi told him, "well then I'll tell you no again, for real."

That made him laugh and she said that it was a little easier to talk to him after that. They were supposed to be friends from that point on, but Jad was acting sus. He started showing up after every one of her classes, offering to carry her books, and giving his jacket up every time she shivered. She felt like they were dating even though they weren't doing anything.

I think Bolly saw all of that and it made her feel like a snail without its shell. Fifi says that she was just trying to be Jad's friend, but she liked him even back then, so it made things harder. But the thing is, every time she got worried about them, Jad would tell her that they were just friends. He even told her about this girl he was planning to ask out. Fifi says he was sketchy about the deets and that every time she asked for her name, he said, "she doesn't go here."

When Jad got the news about my death, he came to her first. Fifi says that he was crying a lot, but when she hugged him, Jad kissed her. She wanted to turn him down, but she didn't. Fifi didn't offer any explanation. She only said that she apologized to my spirit and asked for forgiveness.

Everything after that was basically how Tiff told me it happened. Fifi and Jad's relationship kept getting heavier and the first time that Jad brought his hand under her shirt was the first time they had sex. Fifi said when it happened, he knew right where to go to get condoms. When she asked him about it later, Jad said that he'd been practicing with them. Like he'd jerk off with them or something which sounds super sus to me.

And yeah I still made out with Jad today, but you don't know what happened with me and Jad on our date, okay! So don't judge me too hard, Diary. I didn't know he was a cheater then.

Sorry, I'm jumping around again!

Fifi asked me how I started dating Jad and I told her. I did make it clear that it we kissed after they broke up. Now that Fifi's had some time to think about it and she had me clarify on some of the dates, she's 100% sure that Jad was lying when he said they weren't together. Because when they broke up, it was kind of sudden and it was the only time they hadn't had sex since the first time.

They also kissed on the day they broke up, which means that he 100% kissed her after he kissed me.

Anyway, I need you to know what happened on my date with Jad, because it puts things in perspective. Or at least I thought it did.

Jad and I did some window shopping before the movie. We just tried on hats and sunglasses and did silly stuff like that. The movie was heavy and it made dinner awkward. We were both in our heads until the cheesesticks came. So I asked him about Fifi. I told him that I'd heard a rumor that they were really sexual, like dry humping on couches and stuff.

He asked me to ask him about it again after we left the restaurant, so I did. Jad started going on about how he loved Fifi, but not in the same way that he loves me. He said that Fifi was like this perfect woman in his mind, that when he thought about a girlfriend and what a girlfriend should look like he would see Fifi. She was basically his dream girl, so he thought that being with her would make him happy.

From the sound of things, Bolly and Jad were closer, but when Bolly asked Jad out, he turned her down. He thought that Bolly was going to break apart if he turned her down, just like I told you before, right? Except Jad was also sure that if he dated Bolly, that Fifi would stop flirting with him and move on to another guy.

"So when I saw you looking at me with tears in yours eyes and your cheeks were flushed, something in my lizard brain panicked. I knew that I had to make a choice, date you and really hurt you, or date Fifi. I liked her, but I kind of always knew it wasn't going to last. I thought that if I started dating Fifi, then you'd get over me."

I started crying. I kissed him a lot and told him that I'd

never get over him.

Jad's reply was precious. "I know that now. Maybe I always did, but I was scared of it before. I didn't want to lose you. If my love for Fifi was a rose, then my love for you is a garden of roses. If one dies, it won't matter, because there's always more of you to love."

And that is so sweet! How could I not kiss him after that? How could I not keep kissing him? If we were at his house when we had that talk, I probably would've gone all the way with him. Like, he's sweet, right? He was with Fifi because he thought I couldn't handle a breakup. Maybe Bolly couldn't have, but I'm not Bolly and I told him that.

Okay, I told him, "I'm not like the Holly you know. If something hurts me, I can get up by myself."

"Because you're a Rainbow Warrior." He smiled.

I still don't know if I can tell him I was or not, so I just kissed him.

Now that I know he's a cheater, I don't know what to do. If he was still dating Fifi when he met me, why didn't he tell me? Was he just walking on eggshells like my parents? Was he planning to break up with her but hadn't yet? No, because Jad said that he broke up with her the moment he found out I was back.

It's starting to drizzle. I better go.

# 48

**February 28**

Lily gave me a pack of condoms at school. She told me to keep them at my house in case something happened. I should've thanked her but I was too freaked by it. I didn't tell her about how Jad cheated on me. I didn't really have any time to be alone with her, we barely had enough time for her to pass over the paraphernalia. Well, now I've got a pack of condoms.

Jad wants to come over, but I told him that I'm busy with homework. I wonder why I didn't tell him that I was meeting Brandon. Whatever, he's the one who started our relationship by lying to me, so I can have a few secrets too. I guess I have an entire childhood full of secrets.

## 49

Brandon's been hiding something from me this entire time. I know that sounds like everyone is lying to everyone, but I think Brandon is exactly who he appears to be.

The second I got into Brandon's sister's car, she started driving fast. I thought that was just how she drives, but Brandon pulled out this pocket mirror and was checking the road. He was checking the road for tails like a spy in a movie.

I picked up my head to look back and he grabbed my arm and shook his head. After we got on the highway, she got up a hundred! She would drive from the far left to the far right and back. Then she took the most random exit and we got off in the middle of the woods. His sister was just like, "Gonna go smoke." And then she took off!

I was like, "dude, is your sister a Nascar driver or something?"

"No, she actually knows how to steer curves."

It was pretty sick.

Then Brandon told me the deal with all the driving and the mirrors: Someone's been following me.

Brandon knew that I wouldn't believe him, so he managed to get a picture of the guy standing outside his car. It was Detective Slauson watching me outside The Gate. It was him alright. The city didn't have the money to shave and train two bears.

"When I first came up to talk to you, I thought it was just your dad watching you, but then one day you told me that your dad was at work. So I followed you. I know I shouldn't have followed you, but I needed to know if you were lying to me or if there was some stranger following you. When you went home, I knew that I needed to get a picture of this guy following you. So every time you went to sit on that rock at night I tried to sneak up on that guy. I was only able to get that picture because it was raining. That man looked into the woods every time a squirrel jumped on a tree. Do you know who he is?"

I nodded.

"Is he dangerous? Are you in any kind of trouble?"

"No. I don't think he'd do anything like that."

Brandon relaxed.

I wanted to tell him about everything. I wanted to break the Oath, but I knew then that I had to keep the secret. You haven't sent anyone because Mr. No-Neck was watching me the entire time. You couldn't send anyone. From the sound of things, Brandon was watching me at night too.

"I'm sorry I was watching you, Holly. I just needed to know if you were in any kind of trouble. If you know why this guy is following you, then that's your business. You obviously didn't tell me about this for a reason. You can keep your secrets."

It felt good to not have to lie to him. "Thank you."

"That man put cameras up in the trees too. I'm pretty sure I could turn the cameras off and make it look like squirrels did it."

"Yes! Oh my gosh golly goodness, Brandon, thank you!" I was so excited I threw my arms around him.

Brandon just laughed and it took him a long time to hug me back. He's not a great hugger. He's a little too boney, but I'm not going to date him so I don't know why it matters. Maybe I'm thinking about it now that I know Jad is a cheater. Is all of this just hormones? Maybe sex would calm things down. Something tells me the opposite is more likely.

We sat in the car and talked about more personal things. I lied about the Rainbow Warriors by using Bolly's story. I did tell him about Wikella and the Magicals, but only that they were make believe. Since I didn't really tell him it doesn't really count. Right, Diary? Please tell me you can still hear me. Brandon's gonna deactivate the cameras so you can send someone. Please send someone to tell me. I could meet you at the bridge, but I can't until I find some way to lose the gorilla.

Brandon is a really cool guy, but I feel sad for him. He's not homeschooled because his parents are weirdos. He was bullied as a kid, like really bad. He's got this big scar on his ribs from where they tripped him down this ravine. There's a bunch of foods he can't eat now because he got a hole in his intestines. They patched it up but the doctors don't want him to take any chances. I guess the kids used to call him dab, because his face looks sideways. Brandon was really tense when he told me that.

He says that if he was brave he could go back to school, but he got really bad panic attacks. When he first moved here, he tried to go to Greenwood High. He felt like he couldn't breathe the entire time. It got so bad that at some point he threw up bile in the middle of class but because he was so scared of kids looking at him, he just swallowed it. He even stayed at school so no one would know something was wrong. I think I'd give up after a week too.

Brandon knows that the kids that tripped him were really disturbed, but he can't talk himself out of the anxiety. He's a diagnosed agoraphobic now. Wikella would've used him for her army if she was still around. She used to find people like that and turn them into monsters, turning their fear into anger. Brandon isn't angry though. He actually sounds sad for his abusers. He was almost crying when he told me about how the guy who tripped him was from a broken home.

I think what happened to Brandon is horrible. If I could transform, I might be able to save him. It's been awhile since I went into the astral realm, but it couldn't hurt to try. I know that it's not strictly speaking necessary, but I hope Queen Nephila will make an exception.

# 50

**March 1**

Brandon says that he fried the cameras. Don't send anyone to my house, but maybe leave a message by The Gate. I'll be there tomorrow. I'm going to talk to Lily about how Jad cheated on me tonight. Wish me luck, Diary.

# 51

Lily wasn't just giving me those condoms as a gift, she was getting rid of them. She quit violin lessons. She ended things with *him* and she's just gonna try to focus on herself for a while. Good for her I guess.

Me? I've already had the isolation and introspection and it didn't sit well with me. Things haven't gotten any less complicated with Jad. It's like every time I talk to anyone about Jad I learn something weird or sus or cringe. What is it this time? Well, he and Lily were almost a thing, which all things considered, I should've guessed.

I mean, I don't feel great about Lily right now, but I know in my heart that I'm going to stop being mad at her at some point. She already apologized and more importantly, she didn't do anything with him when she had the chance. That's what's important. The same can't be said about Fifi. Sure I was dead, but the slut couldn't even wait a week? Was my body even cold?

I don't know. I guess I'm not supposed to be mad about how every girl in school had a chance to be with Jad before me. Fifi tried. Lily told Jad that she couldn't hurt me, but she still kissed him.

Yeah, that's the thing about my friend. As good of a friend as she is, Lily still kissed Jad, so I guess all of her anger and resentment makes a lot more sense now. I should just accept the simple truth that I'm not that important of a person and I never really was. When I think about it, I had to die to get anyone to be nice to me. I literally had to do magic to become relevant, so why am I ever even surprised when my friends stab me in the back, or when my boyfriend apparently chose me last out of every girl in the world.

I know that you want me to tell you about all of my lies and to let you know what's going on in my life, but I'm just so over all of these twists. The only thing keeping me in this world right now is the fact that I don't even have the wand and the key anymore. That was the one thing I was supposed to be good at, being a Rainbow Warrior. Now I can't even do that right. I can't even be a messiah right. Everyone online hates me. Twitter, Insta, Tiktok, and even my random as fudge covered cookies Tumblr account are all dead now.

You can't control me, Diary. I don't have to tell you about shishido peppers if I don't go to sleep.

# 52

**March 2**

Morning. Did you send anyone through the gate? Yeah, I didn't think so. I don't even know why I'm playing by the book anymore. One swear word and I can never go back anyway. When I think about it, that's really jank. One swear word and I'm out. Seriously? I've been thinking about it and no one has a zero strike system. How am I supposed to learn how to forgive Lily, or Fifi, or Jad, when you and the Royals literally never forgive anyone? With all of your power and wisdom, none of you taught me how to forgive. Is that some agent of wickedness too, like everything else in the human experience? Am I already blacklisted because I kissed a boy?

I'm so mad at you, Diary. I'm mad at you and all the Magicals. If Detective Slauson is watching over my house, all you have to do is turn him into mince meat. I've seen what Captain Aligator can do to a human body when he sets his mind to it. I know how deadly a 12 foot wide orb weaving spider can be. Princess Platypus is like 500 years old, right? You're trying to tell me she can't kill one human? I didn't think so.

I don't know why I keep writing to you. I don't know why I'm keeping up with the Oath. Until you send someone, I'm not writing you. You can't keep me from sleeping forever. Eventually I'll get so tired that I'll pass out. You wouldn't kill me to keep my promise.

# 53

I'm sorry.

I'm sorry about a lot of things, Diary. I've been selfish. Everything's been about me. Maybe it always has been. I think this is why I needed to come here. Without Jad, I never would've gotten out of this cycle. I would've slid right back to thinking that literally everyone is against me and that they all hate me.

Queen Nephila not caring about me? You? Lily? None of that makes any sense. Lily gave him one kiss, that's it. She kissed him once and then she took it back. She left Future Authors Club to stay away from Jad. She loved that club. She's wanted to be an author since she was eight and now she doesn't even write. And you and the Royals have always been there for me. I know you're trying to get through. I know you are. I'm sorry.

I've been off my meds, Diary. I stopped taking them a few days back. They were making me manic. My mind was all over the place, you saw how I was. I thought that it was going to ruin things here, but I was wrong. Before I was used to having all these bigly thoughts, but I got a little bit of a break from holding those feelings back and suddenly it's like I'm a pupper all over again.

Lily didn't notice. Mom and Dad didn't notice, but Jad did. He knows me better than anyone. He loves me. He really loves me and he was willing to hurt our relationship to ask me about my meds. He was scared, Diary. He was literally scared of me because all this talk about him kissing other girls shut my brain off.

I feel so bad about getting mad at Lily. She didn't come to school today. She said that she was just sick when I texted her right now. I guess she has the right to lie to me, I've been so wild lately.

I'm gonna call the hospital tomorrow about trying to

change my meds. Jad helped me look up some stuff about anti-anxiety medication and they're not supposed to cause mood swings like I was having. Jad said I might need antidepressants instead, but I think it might be worse. I've been looking up my symptoms and I might need some antipsychotics. That means I'm really bad, Diary. That means that I'm close to being indistinguishable from Wikella's puppers. The biggest problem is that I can't actually be honest with my therapist because she'll think that I'm also suffering from fantasies when I'm not.

I guess I can't really worry about that right now. I mean I can, but the worrying doesn't help me. I need to relax and focus on my breathing. It was easier to do that when I was with Jad. When he holds me it's like the entire world disappears. I feel like I'm myself when I'm with him, but the mask I wear normally is really starting to choke me.

I got Jad's side of Lily's story about them almost hooking up in freshman year. It wasn't anything. They got close. They both kind of liked each other, but they both agreed not to get together because they didn't want to hurt me. That's kind of it. Jad says she kissed him one time when they were just hanging out but nothing came of it.

It sounded worse when Lily was talking about it, but that's probably because she felt so guilty and I didn't help. I make everyone around me nervous. Sometimes I start conversations by screaming at people. Why do I do that?

I'm so tired of myself. I was supposed to be better here and I'm not. I stopped taking the meds and I turned into myself. I thought I'd gotten better but maybe it was the meds all along.

## 54

**March 3**

I'm staying home today. I was going to go to Lily's house but she went to school. I don't want to go back to school until the meds are making me a good person again. I guess it can take another week to get readjusted, but it might take as little as three days. I feel better than I did yesterday. Thanks for letting me sleep last night, Diary. I probably lied to someone about something yesterday, but I honestly don't remember what I lied about.

School was fine. I thought it was the worst day ever because I was all agro about Lily, but I was flipping about little things. I poked my gums with my toothbrush. I spilled OJ on my shirt. I dropped my history book and the pages landed in mud tracks. But honestly all of that stuff wasn't even a big deal. I ended up being such a bitter cookie that I blew Jad off at lunch. I'm so glad he came over yesterday and we talked. He told me that he didn't kiss Lily back because he knew he didn't really like her, he just thought she was cute, and she is. Lily's a beautiful woman. What kind of a girlfriend would I be if I got mad at Jad for things that he did before we even started dating?

Mom's at work and it's pretty boring right now. I'm so bored that I'm actually doing homework. I think I'm going to invite Brandon over.

# 55

I fell asleep on Brandon's arm. I drooled all over his shirt and he didn't even wake me. I made him promise to wake me if that ever happened again. I don't want him to be afraid of me. He says he isn't but he's kind of afraid of everyone. He's a really cool guy. I was thinking about his situation and then I had a cool idea: what if he and Lily were dating? Then she wouldn't be tempted to go back to sleazy college guy and Brandon could build up his confidence and go back to a real school.

I just wish that I was popular enough to host a party. I guess I could but it would be lame if it was just Jad, Lily, Brandon, and me. If I did that then it would totally feel like a double date and I don't want them to think that I'm trying to get them together, even though I am. I still haven't told Brandon about Jad, but I really don't think he's interested in me. He was just trying to help me the whole time, we were never gonna be a thing.

# 56

Jad surprised me by coming over!

We only got to be alone for like thirty minutes before Mom came home, but those were some hot thirty minutes. I was honestly starting to think about using those condoms when I heard the front door open. I was going to wait until I got on the new medication, or at least until the anti-anxiety pills kicked in, but I don't know now. Jad only kissed Fifi because he was going to break up with her. They "kissed hello." Jad and I do that all the time. I guess the thing that I should be the most mad at him about was him lying about breaking things off with Fifi before he did, but he was worried about me. I had just killed myself.

# 57

**March 6**


I'm gonna go to Tiff's house this Friday for sure. Jad said he would go too. I want to pick out a cool outfit, but I'm not sure what.

I apologized to Lily at school, for like the fourth time, but she was whatever about it. Lily didn't even seem to care. I didn't even see her at lunch. Amber said that Lily gets like that sometimes. We kind of talked about meds and how most of us were on one kind of drug or another. Indra said that she's actually on birth control because she gets really bad cramps and it evened out her moods. I wonder if I could go on birth control without Mom thinking that I was going to have sex. It might be a little too late for that now.

Oh, I told my bio teacher that I forgot my homework, even though I didn't do it. She didn't care. The teachers really are going to give me A's no matter what.

# 58

**March 8**

Ugh! Right when things felt like they were finally starting to settle down again, this happens?

I guess I should start by thanking you, Diary. You finally sent someone, I just didn't expect it to be the other Jaden. Does that mean I have to call my boyfriend, Bad, now? No. I'm not doing that. The Jad from my world, World A, is Aden and Jad's my boyfriend and that's the way it's going to be.

Aden caught me on my way out to school. He looked so different. His hair was almost down to his nose and he had stubble. I'd never seen him like that before. Where did he even get that brown bomber jacket from?

So Aden shows up at my door looking like an extra from the VA commercials, and just walks in. He didn't even say anything to me. He just looked at me like I was in trouble and walked in. How the eff did he even know my rents were gone? Because he's been stalking me. Good to know Aden hasn't lost his romantic streak.

Mister heartbreaker, the guy who probably kissed Aily, World A Lily, stomped over to the kitchen and started eating all our leftovers.

I was like, "how'd you get here?"

"Finn."

Like, what? Finn brought him here. How did Finn get him to our world? He told me he threw the ruby wand into the ocean. I had a million questions and Aden didn't answer any of them. He was busy choking down food luck a duck! When he finished his third meal, he sat there with his eyes closed and held his hands out. They were shaking. I watched them slow and he let out the nastiest burp I'd heard in my life. Then this gross, grungy, soup kitchen reject version of Aden walked up the stairs of my house.

"I'm going to go to school if you don't talk to me."

"Fine, I'll wait for you here."

That pissed me off. My house wasn't a fudge scooping hotel! He needed to tell me what was going on. He owed me that!

"Hey! You can't just go through my house and take whatever you want."

"It's not your house."

Can you believe he would say that to me?! "What the fricker frack are you talking about? This is my house. Those are my towels! Why are you grabbing towels?"

He walked into my parent's bathroom and started stripping. "Douglas Adams said I need to. What do you think I'm doing?"

I turned around. The first time I saw Jad naked, any Jad, it was not going to be like that! "Jad, you can't just come in here, eat my food, and use my shower!"

"Wash my clothes." He ordered me like a dog and started the water before I could object.

I was so mad and confused that I didn't even know what to do. His clothes were rank though. They smelled like a monkey's catapult. I can't believe I did it, but I threw his clothes into the wash and started a load of laundry. I got one of Dad's old band shirts that he never wears and some boxers and khakis. I hadn't realized it before, but Dad's actually about the same size as Jad.

I haven't gone in to check on him. I just put his clean clothes on the toilet and I didn't peek! Why is he taking so long in there? Something tells me I don't want to know the answer. Is he starting the shower a third time?!

## 59

Aden's asleep on my bed. Nothing happened. Not that I would have sex with this Jaden anyway. He's like homeless loser Jaden and he's a real jerk chicken cooker.

When his majesty finally got out of the shower, he tossed the three towels at me like I was his maid.

"Why'd you give me these?"

"To wash them." He walked over to my room and entered without knocking.

I tossed the towels on my parent's bed. "Hey! You can't go in there!"

"Where are they?"

"Where are what? Hey! What are you doing?" Aden was going through my drawers so I slapped his arm. "Stay out of my stuff!"

"They're not your stuff," he said again.

It made me so mad that I couldn't even think of a comeback.

Aden glanced over at my rent's room. "You're really not going to wash those towels, huh?"

"No. I'm not your maid or your servant or whatever."

"You're not telling me to [f-word] off even though you clearly want to, so you haven't broken your Oath to those psycho cartoon characters you call friends. You also remember me, so you should remember how important it is to not draw attention to us being here. Do I really have to point out how reckless it is to leave towels that I soiled?"

I grumbled and put the towels in the washer. I was seriously doing his laundry. I'd never been so mad at Aden.

"I'll ask you again, where is it?"

"Where's what?"

He walked up and touched my hips. His eyes were serious

and his brows were broody and deep. Maybe his new look wasn't so bad after all. I barely even noticed that Aden was frisking me.

"Where's the wand and key, Holly?"

My eyes drooped.

"Holly."

"They were stolen."

"Stolen?"

"I stored them under a rock and a homicide detective found them."

Aden sat on my bed, groaned, and fell back on the comforters.

"Why are you being like this? You're just taking everything you want and giving me all these short answers. Finn got you here, how does that make any sense?"

"I've been living in the woods, Holly. I haven't had anything good to eat in three days and I haven't had a good place to sleep in...I don't know how long."

"Okay, but can't we slow down and talk? We obvi have to catch up."

He scowled at me and then dropped back on the bed.

"What?!"

"Let's see. You disappeared without telling anyone so Lily, me, your parents, and the entire school thought you'd been kidnapped, raped, and killed. When I finally found out what really happened to you, I had to negotiate with a fifteen-foot long cartoon serpent to prove that I'm not a 'pupper,' whatever the [f-word] that is. In between those lovely 'trials,' they put me on a rack, had me quartered, and made me stand in a [g-word] [d-word] iron maiden! After I was thoroughly and sufficiently broken, they finally told me what happened. That you faked your death and took over the life of a version of you that killed herself, all so you could date me! Am I missing anything?!"

My mouth fell open. I felt so numb.

"Yeah, I didn't think so."

I felt tears coming and he snapped at me.

"Go cry somewhere else!"

I closed the door and cried in the hall. When I got back, he was asleep on my bed. He's still sleeping there now.

When I asked you to send help, I didn't think this was the kind of help you were going to send. Why did Judge Cobra have him tortured? He's just a regular human! You should've just let him through. I kept telling you that I needed help, didn't I? If you see Princess Platypus and Judge Cobra, you tell them that there will be punishments for what they did to Aden!

## 60

Aden woke up in better spirits. I made him a sandwich and some tea and he promised not to yell at me again.

"I'd never seen a mother lose her daughter before and I don't want to see it again. Not as long as I live. She was a wreck, Holly. She couldn't even make herself a sandwich without dropping something or breaking down in tears. Your dad basically turned into an alcoholic. I kept having to turn him down for a drink. He didn't care that I was sixteen, he just wanted an excuse to not drink alone, but he stopped caring real fast.

"I was there every day after you disappeared, Holly. Lily was too. We couldn't understand why you would just take off like that. I thought someone had you. I looked all over town for some clues, we all did. The entire school mobilized to go out looking for you and nobody found so much as a scrunchy.

"Lily wasn't sleeping, not that any of us were, but I think it hit Lily harder because she was the last one who talked to you. We both blamed ourselves, I want you to know that. I was running everywhere I could to try and find you, and I only stopped because a police officer dragged me back home. I was running myself to death and Lily was calling everyone she could, but she was calling everyone who knew Sasha.

"Sasha was our only clue on where to go. I thought Lily was delusional, but the more I thought about it, the more it made sense. We were thinking there was some kind of child napping operation going on in town. Maybe you were being sold in LA or Chicago, we had no idea. We imagined every possible fate for you and mourned your death a hundred times. Then Lily got in touch with Finn.

"He didn't want to talk to us at first. He acted like he was barely even friends with you and Sasha. It was only after you'd been declared legally dead that he finally came back. That's when he pulled back the curtain.

"It was insane. I didn't believe it. How could I? But the more Finn told us about these cartoon caretakers and magical adventures, the more Lily started putting pieces together. You'd always been so guarded about your past and she'd seen your scars in gym class, and of course there were your stories you'd submitted to Future Authors Club.

"The Rainbow Warriors were real and the seven of you saved the world from some evil witch named Wikella. It was all so absurd, but that was your life. I think the thing that finally made me believe Finn was when he told us about the Oath. Five little laws that came to define your life: kiss at every rainbow, never reveal the truth of magic, never reveal the Magicals, never show magic to the ignorant, and you couldn't swear.

"Everyone I knew that didn't swear always had some exception. One word or phrase that they let themselves say, but you didn't. You had your little Hollyisms that you'd say instead like, bitter cookie, and fudge with nuts. Nobody else talked like that. It was like you came up with your own words or you were from a different world.

"Finn said that he broke the Oath a long time ago so he could never go back, but if we were pure of heart we could go through the gate and bring you back. I wasn't sure I wanted to meet giant cartoon animals with silly little hats and enough magic to turn me into a smoking pile of ash, but Lily was all about it. Once she found out that you'd left us on purpose, she was going to drag you back.

"When it came time for us to step through the gate, Lily couldn't follow me through. She'd done something she wasn't proud of and I didn't ask her about it. With everything we'd been through, I honestly didn't care. It was scary though. Lily's one of the kindest people I've ever known and suddenly I knew for a fact that I was pure and she wasn't. It made no sense.

"Now that I've met King Walrus and Queen Nephila, I get it. I thought they were funny or cute when I read your stories.

You didn't tell me that the king sucked up four-foot large oyster people into his mouth while he served the court, or that Queen Nephila kept her latest victim close by to take a casual slurp from her victim's blood. If those were your magical saviors and heroes, I don't know how you survived childhood."

"We thought they were funny," I mumbled.

Aden gave a long sigh before he started up again. "I was roughed up and tortured by eight-foot tall cartoons. They cut off my arm and then magicked it back and laughed the entire time! I don't know why they finally believed me, I must've said the right word or phrase or something. They brought me to court and announced that a feast would be held to welcome the friend of the Noble Emerald Warrior. They brought up my torture like it was the funniest thing in the world and all just water under the bridge.

"As weird as all of that was, I definitely wasn't expecting a giant platypus woman with razor thin eyelashes to come into my room and try to seduce me. She had me undressed and halfway into her bill before I screamed about being in love. I don't know why it came to me, it just seemed like the right kind of nonsense logic to use against a bunch of psychotic cartoons.

"The next day His and Her Royal Majesties knighted me and sent me to come get the wand and key."

I asked, "They don't want me back?"

Aden shook his head. "They said that you were happy here. I honestly don't know if I care at this point. I just want to get the wand and key and be done with this. How tough is this detective guy?"

"He's got a body from Gears of War and the mind of Holmes."

Aden fell back into his deep brooding.

After a time I asked him, "What happened after you came out The Gate?"

"I knew that I probably couldn't go to you because you might be with your boyfriend." He looked over my outfit for maybe the first time. There was scorn in his eyes. "So I went to

Lily. She took the day off and we talked about what you've been doing for the past seven weeks. At some point her mom came home and I had to leave through the back. I've been hiding in the woods waiting for your tail to disappear. I take it that's Detective Chainsaw Gun?"

"Slauson, yeah."

"Great, so-"

There was a knock on the front door. Before Aden could run off to hide, we heard my Jad on the other side. Well, we heard my Jad Jad. The Jad from this world. My boyfriend. Ugh! I really am going to have to call him Baden, aren't I? Fine. Baden, native of World B, knocked on the front door.

I opened the door, but used my foot to keep him from coming in.

"Hey."

"Hi, Jad!" I leaned in and kissed him hello.

Aden was watching me with his arms crossed.

"What's going on? Why can't you let me in?"

I shook my head. "I'm really sick. I don't think I should."

He chuckled. "Seriously. Hey, you look like you've been crying." Baden brushed my hair behind my ear. "You know you can talk to me, right?"

"I do." I kissed him.

He kissed back with passion and almost pushed me inside, but I stopped him.

"I mean it, Jad. You can't come in."

"Are you gonna be at school tomorrow?"

"I don't know. I'll let you know tonight, okay?"

We kissed again. I would've kept it going but I had an audience that refused to go hide. I let him go and the second he was gone, Aden was watching his time clone from the cracks in the front room curtains.

Aden waited for him to be completely gone before asking me. "Was it worth it?"

"What?"

"The pain you caused your mom and dad and everyone in

school. Was it worth it just to make him your boyfriend?"

"Do you honestly expect me to answer that?"

Aden shook his head. "I can't believe I thought I knew you."

"You did know me. We have everything in common, Jad. We were perfect for each other but you were too busy fantasizing about Fifi!"

"Is that why you're dressed like her?" He muttered but he muttered it loud enough for me to hear. He wanted me to hear it.

"I do not dress like her!"

"Right." He rolled his eyes. Wow, so cool! "I don't even know why I'm talking to you about this! All that matters is getting the wand and the key back."

I asked him, "Do you have the key with you?"

"No, I hid it."

I couldn't believe what I was hearing.

"I didn't hide it under a rock! It's safe."

"I hope it is or you might actually be stuck here."

Aden went upstairs to get his stuff. "I'm gonna be back here tonight. We'll get what we need from this detective and then I can take it back to the Magicals and you can live psycholy-ever-after."

"That won't work. He's too strong and too smart. We need to go back to your world."

Aden wasn't about to let that fly. "My world?"

"Our world." It was my turn to roll my eyes, but he deserved it. "You know what I mean!"

"Why do we need to go back?"

"Finn still has his magic wand, I know he does. If we can get it back, then we can poof the detective and set everything right."

"Poof?"

I shrugged.

Aden laughed this sick bitter judgmental laugh. "You're actually going to kill him."

"It's worse than you think! He knows about magic. We

can't let him live."

"Why, because it'll break your little oath? Why do you care so much about going back to the Magicals? Isn't this your dream life?"

I went quiet and Aden went for the door.

"Right. Why would you start being honest with me now?"

"I was always honest!"

Aden let out a cruel laugh.

"As honest as I could be."

"You know something, Holly, you were never as good of a liar as you thought you were. You think that we had so much in common and that we were perfect for each other, but we weren't. I never had a clue who you were and I knew that about you. I tried so hard to get you to open up about your childhood and talk about the friends you used to have—that you clearly weren't over—and you never told me anything. You've been fake since the first day I met you. Why would I fall in love with that? Even if I did, how could I ever make you happy?"

"You do!"

He arched his cruel little brow to mock me.

"I mean, the other you."

"You mean the me that was falling for a you that killed herself? Are we talking about that me? Whatever you're feeling now with him, it won't last. I don't know who he is, but if he's anything like me he's not going to be happy with a liar. He's happy you're back. He might be happy to kiss you and go to whatever baseball metaphor you've been to with him, but eventually all of those chemicals in his brain will go away and he'll realize that he's in a relationship with a complete stranger."

He's wrong. I know he's wrong! He said those things to hurt me.

Aden went for the door again.

"Come back Saturday night."

"Why then?"

"I have a party to go to and I want to tell people I'm leaving for a while."

Aden almost started yelling at me again, but he closed his eyes and let it all out with a single sigh. "Well, it's good to know you finally met friends that you actually care about."

"Jad."

He slammed the door on his way out.

What am I supposed to do with that, Diary? I'm tired and my hand hurts. Hopefully, school won't be a total drag. I can't believe I'm gonna have to leave everyone. It'll be worth it to get some answers from Finn, though. I knew he was lying to me. I've known he was lying from the first time he came up with his "you need professional help" lie. When I meet him I'm going to find out why he's been lying all this time. Then I'm going to come back here and lose my virginity to the man that loves me and there isn't a single thing that hobo can do about it!

# 61

**March 9**


I want to tell my parents about my trip, but I can't let them know before I'm gone or they might try to stop me. I'm going to leave them a note. It's the best I can do. I'm honestly not sure what to tell them. I don't know how long I'm going to be gone. Maybe two weeks. Please let the Royals know that I'm coming. I need to be able to get through the Magical Castle quickly. Though I have more than a few things to say to them.

I can't believe they tortured Aden. He's my friend, shouldn't that be enough? I guess it might've been if I walked in with him, but if I had, Aden wouldn't have needed to come here in the first place.

Gotta go, Aden showed up.

# 62

**March 10**

Tiff's party is in a couple hours. What do you wear to a first party that might be your last? Tiff's at an away game, so no one really wants to go see them play. I might've gone if I had a car, but I got too much to do.

Bily and I talked at lunch. She was practically waiting for me at my locker. She didn't have to say anything. I knew from the look on her face that she wanted to talk to me about Aden. We went to an alley between the bungalows. She looked like she wanted to slap me.

"I met up with the other Jaden," I told her.

"I ran into him last night."

"Ah."

Then we were back to a drawn out awkward silence. She was in so much pain.

"What kind of a monster just steals somebody's life?"

"I didn't steal-"

"Then what would you call it?!"

"I'm still your friend, Lily. All of your memories with Holly, I had those memories too."

"I don't think you did. The Holly that I knew never would've stolen somebody's life. They wouldn't have left-" Bily cut herself off. She couldn't finish her thought with the tears threatening to come back.

I tried to comfort her.

Bily smacked my arm. "Don't [f-word] touch me! I should've known something was up when you never brought up the Magicals! I just thought that you'd finally let go, but that wasn't it at all. She..." She fell back against the wall and started to cry.

It broke my heart that I couldn't reach out and hug her. I wanted to take away her pain.

"This is worse. This is so much worse than what I had to deal with before." She said between sobs. "She's gone and it's like you're wearing her face! I have to accept the fact that my best friend is dead, that she took her life, and I'll never really know why! And you..." Lily shoved me back against the wall. "You come in here like a [g-word] [d-word] ghoul and steal her life! What was it for?! Why would you hurt us like this? Why would you hurt me! Don't you care about how your friends feel?"

"Of course I do, Lily! That's why I came-"

"Bull[s-word]! You still left me! You left them to think that you're dead, but you weren't! You ran off to act like you'd come back from the dead and for what? Why would you put Jaden, your Jaden, through all of that?! Why would you hurt your Lily like this?!"

She pushed me again, at least once more. I didn't try to stop her. I wouldn't have stopped her if she slapped me or punched me. She deserved some catharsis, no matter how small.

"Answer me!"

"It's like-"

"Speak up!"

I was so scared and ashamed that my hands were shaking. "I wasn't happy. I hadn't been happy in a very long time. I was different. Everyone else, they had normal school drama and stuff with their parents and their friends to worry about. I'd seen people die. I'd been a part of their deaths. I walked into the minds of rapists and killers and saw all their deepest worst thoughts and I came out of it and had to pretend that everything was okay and it wasn't.

"Nothing was okay with me. I wasn't just a rabbit with the wrong coat, Lily, I was a rabbit who'd come in from the worst winter of her life--one that lasted years. I'd seen so much of humanity and evil and I didn't relate to anything anyone was saying. Every single time someone at school talked about their drama at home or the things their friends did, I kept thinking to myself, 'wait until you grow up, it's only going to get worse.'

"I mean, all the stuff with school and parents taking away their rights? Everyone honestly thinks that's as bad as this gets?! There isn't a world of freedom for us after graduation. The collars are tighter, the cages are smaller, and the tricks we have to perform are cruel. Some people get to have a happily ever after, but most don't. Most people stay alive because they just aren't willing to end it."

I was screaming and crying. I'd kind of freaked Bily out. I had to wipe my nose off on my jacket. Gross, but I didn't have anything else. I felt that way too, like I didn't have anything. I'd never been able to tell someone what it was like and now that I'd said it to Bily, it hadn't brought us closer together. She was looking at me not just like I was a stranger, but like she'd never known me in the first place--any version of me.

Lily took her time asking, "what does that have to do with coming here?"

I shook my head. "Just forget it."

"I deserve to know! If you think we don't have a future, then why did you even come here? Why did you take the life of my best friend, if you have no hope?"

I didn't want to tell her. Sharing my isolation didn't make either of us feel any better. My lies are supposed to be to keep other people from worrying, but maybe it's not that simple. Maybe we know that the truth about how miserable we are isn't worth talking about because there's nothing anyone can do about it. It's like in Majora's Mask. No one wants to look at the moon.

"I'm going back to my world. I'm gonna find Finn, and we're going to come back here to get my wand and key. Once we do, I'm gonna go live with the Magicals. It won't be right away. Maybe I'll be back here for a month, maybe I'll wait until graduation, but one day I'm going to leave Earth and never look back. I've seen what I have waiting for me after graduation. I know what it means to be an adult, I know what the life of a human really looks like, and I don't want that."

"Not good enough. Why here, Holly? Why did you come to this world if you had a Jaden and a Lily and an entire life of your own?" When I didn't answer right away she snapped, "answer me!"

"Sex. I wanted to have sex and get drunk for real and I wanted to have a boyfriend and know what it was like to be loved by a human. They don't have that there in the Magical Castle. They don't feel love. They don't have souls like we do. Leaving Earth meant that I'd never be able to do those things."

"Why here, Holly?"

I couldn't look her in the eyes when I told her the truth. "Because she killed herself."

"I don't understand. You basically killed yourself when you left your world."

"I wanted to see how much everyone would miss me. I-"

"You wanted everyone to be happy that you were still alive." Bily sounded like she was gonna push me again.

"Yeah."

She paced. "That's sick. You're sick! I can't believe you would do that!"

"Are you trying to tell me you wouldn't do the same thing in my position?!"

"No!"

"So if you had the power to make everyone like you again, you wouldn't use it?"

"No, Holly! That's only something you would do!"

"I don't think it is! My life was going nowhere, Lily. My parents forgot I existed and only ever talked to me to check up on my grades, which were terrible. My crush was spending all his time drooling over a slut. My best friend was so sick of hearing me whine, that she actually told me that she couldn't do sad every day."

Bily lowered her eyes for a moment. "You were a wreck."

"I was and things weren't getting any better, but they are now. Things are better because everyone realized how much they missed me. People take love for granted. We see the same people everyday and their faces aren't special anymore, it's just another fixture in our sad lives. But when I came back, my parents stopped wasting all their money on small things to make them less miserable and actually took care of their daughter. Jad left that slut and came to be with me, because we were always in love and only after I was gone, did he appreciate me!"

"Why didn't you just stay in the Magical Castle for a month before going back to your world?"

I didn't want to say it out loud. I didn't even really want to tell you about it. I guess I don't need to tell you now, because I told Bily the truth. But maybe you've already figured it out.

"I wanted a backup," I admitted.

"A backup?"

"If things went weird here, if Jad didn't like this Holly or if something weird happened with you, I needed to have another world to come back to."

Lily was seething. "You were using us as a dry run?! This whole world was a playground for you to test our reactions. That's why you cared so much about why I was upset with you?"

"Yes."

She didn't slap me then. She punched me. I saw her shoulders move and I stood there and took it. I'm surprised at how hard Lily punched me. I've got some swelling now. I've never had a black eye before, but I do now. I can understand why Lily was upset and I can even understand why she punched me, but I didn't say anything that's wrong, or even short sighted.

I've had this power for years and I haven't used it at all. I could've traveled to a world virtually identical to mine and kissed Jad, just to see how he'd react. At any point in time, I could've slipped into Jad's mind and found his deepest desires. I didn't want that. I didn't want to trick Jad into loving me. I wanted him to love me for who I am and he did. He fell in love with me, but he talked himself out of being with me because I wore drab pants and no appeal shirts and couldn't be bothered to wear makeup. I was always beautiful, but I didn't put in the effort. That's why Fifi took him from me.

I didn't live my life well and it took me coming back from the dead to see how wrong I was about how I lived my life. Yes, I don't have my backup anymore because Finn fudge packed it, but I don't need that backup. Baden is in love with me. He left Fifi for me. Aden, he doesn't matter anymore. He can go be an angry hobo in World A. Maybe that Fifi is into that stuff.

I hate that Aden said I dress like Fifi now. I don't. She wears pinks and pastels and puts on dresses with funorific paisleys. I wear autumn colors and I don't even own any spaghetti string tops. I'm not walking around school with my powdered cleavage pushed up so all the freshies can jerk off to me in the bathroom. He liked Fifi because she dressed like a whore, so who is he to attack my outfit anyway?!

# 63

I don't know how it happened. We were drinking and dancing and having a good time and I wanted to sit down. Next thing I know, we're in the guest bedroom with the door locked. He was blushed and sweaty and I had to kiss his deliciousness. Things got hot really fast and his hands went from my thigh to between my legs and it felt good. Goodness golly gracious it felt good! I could barely keep kissing with how he was touching me.

When he whispered into my ear, "I want you," I wanted him too. I touched him through his jeans. I'd felt him against my hip or my leg, but this was something else entirely. Once I touched him, everything was real. It was going to happen.

He started kissing me like crazy! His hands and lips were all over me. I helped him take off my shirt and I got his shirt off so fast that I missed a button. Now his shirt is missing the button too! I was so horny. Nothing could keep me from putting our bare skin together. I was touching him, not just his neck and the small of his back, but I was touching his erection. He unzipped and I started rubbing him through his boxers.

I could feel his warmth. The first time he pulsed I thought I'd made him come. We laughed about it. I'm not ashamed to admit that I was disappointed when I thought he had come. It was nice to see him laughing and smiling at me. We were just happy and in the moment. Just like before, the whole party had disappeared, and it was just my boyfriend and me. That changed when he took his pants off and the condom was in his hand.

I don't need candles and George Michael's "Careless Whisper," to lose my virginity, but the thought of it happening while I was half drunk at Tiff's party didn't make me feel good. I don't care that people think Baden and I are already doing it, but I don't want them to actually hear us doing the deed. If I bled from him entering me I was either going to have to clean the sheets or leave that mess for Tiff.

Baden had the condom in his hand when he asked, "do you want to put it on?"

I grabbed his hand with the condom in it. I held it until he could see the change in my eyes. "I do, but I don't want to put it on tonight."

"Are you okay? Is it the alcohol?" He didn't sound pushy, I promise you, Diary. He was worried about me more than anything.

"It's here. It's the timing."

Jad looked around at the guest room like he'd only just seen it for the first time. There was a picture of Jesus Christ looking at us. "Yeah, this maybe isn't the best place for us to do it the first time."

"Are you going to be alright?" I tried to sound mature, but I might've blushed when I asked him, "Are you going to get blue balls?"

He laughed. "Um...I don't think so." He gave me a peck on the cheek. "I'll take care of it."

"You mean like..."

He did a masturbation hand gesture. It was cute and funny.

"Okay."

"Do you want to stay and watch?"

I did but I shook my head and got dressed. I got by the door, turned around and whispered, "can I see it?"

And I did. It was kind of far away, but I liked it. Something about seeing him naked and erect stirred my loins. He was horny for me. I wanted to stay there and model for him. I wanted to see that ecstasy in his face grow. I wanted those cute red cheeks to smile while he came. But the sight of him stroking brought things back to reality. I locked the door on my way out.

# 64

Getting drunk at the party wasn't as big of a deal as I thought it would be. My head was just a little hazy, but I could still move. I guess it felt like I was in water sometimes because my body moved slow. We were two drinks in when we started dancing. Everyone was calling the drinks screwdrivers, but it was just vodka poured into orange juice. I always thought it was hard to make cocktails.

I tried drinking a beer after I went outside to let Baden take care of his balls. It tasted really bad, but it was cold. The perfect drink for how I was feeling. I wonder if people drink beer because they don't want to get drunk, because it worked for me. No one asked about where Baden and I went and no one brought him up when I left him behind. People were chilling and having fun and I didn't have to talk to anyone if I didn't want to.

I ended up cooling off on the balcony and I talked to Allie a little bit about Fifi. I guess she's doing okay, but she's still sour about everything that happened. Allie said she was seeing a therapist and was probably going to start taking antidepressants. I wondered if she was going to see the same therapist, but that would be too much coincidence for one life.

Baden was all smiles when he came back. He wrapped his arm around me, kissed me on the cheek and told me, "thank you."

"For what?"

"Being honest. I'm glad that wasn't our first time."

"I'm a little disappointed," I admitted.

"Just a little?"

I giggled. "A lot. That was hot. I liked what you were doing with your fingers."

"I liked what you were doing with yours."

We made out a little, but then it threatened to get intense again so we went and played cards with Tiff.

She was really sad about me leaving. Tiff gave me the biggest hug goodbye. She squeezed me so tight I thought I might choke. I promised her that I was going to come back. Tiff called me her "best [b-word]." It was sweet.

I told Baden about my trip too. He thought we were gonna go somewhere together and got a little mad when I told him that he couldn't come with me.

"Is this because we almost...? Because I just drank too much. I didn't mean for things to happen like they did, I swear, Holly."

I kissed him slow and tender. "No, Jad. I'm not mad about that. What we did in the guest room, it was... I had a lot of fun and I definitely want to do that again. But I was already planning to leave, that's why I said this was bad timing. I didn't want us to start having sex right before I left for two weeks."

"You said it was going to be ten days."

"I don't know if it's going to be ten days. It might be three weeks, I might be done in five, but this is something that I need to do." I kissed him again. "Lily gave me most of a box of condoms. When I get back, we're gonna go through them all. Okay?"

We made out a little, but had to stop when Tiff came out to drive us home.

I hate that I have to leave them all. Everyone but Bily has been really sad to see me go again. Her friends have kind of sided with me about my black eye. I didn't want that to happen. I didn't want there to be any drama about it, but everyone saw us talking by the bungalows, so they put together what happened. I tried to explain it from my side the best that I could, but it was hard without sharing deets. I just kept telling them that Bily was still mad about me killing myself. Eventually, I did tell them that Bily didn't want to be my friend anymore, so my eye was kind of a breakup mark. They got it, but they seemed to think that Bily was the one being a bitter cookie.

I didn't want to take Bily's friends. Maybe my time away will fix that. I don't know. I can't remember if I told any other lies.

# 65

**March 11**

Okay, among the top ten worst things to wake up to, Aden's scruffy face is high on that list. He was like, "it's Saturday, let's go."

"I'm a human. I need food, shower, a backpack full of clothes..."

"You're not packed?!"

"No, why would I be packed?"

"You're not getting it. Detective Slauson isn't outside. I don't know why he isn't here, but if we're going to enter The Gate we need to get a move on."

I gave up the wrist watch my Uncle gave me for eighth grade graduation. "Just meet me at the gate in two hours."

"Two hours?!"

"I still need to say goodbye and write a note to my parents."

He rolled his eyes, but then he took the watch and left. I don't even know how he got inside, it's not like Mom and Dad forget to lock up when they leave. And my keys are where I left them.

I need to write a letter to my parents, Diary. I have no clue what I'm gonna say. "Leaving for two weeks. Don't look for me or call the police. I love you, bye." Yeesh. Let's hope this all works out.

# 66

We're still waiting for King Walrus and Queen Nephila to see us, Diary. If they're talking to you can you tell them to hurry up?

I met up with Brandon before we left. I needed him to stay away from the gate until I got back and I wanted to say goodbye and thank him. My trip was only really possible because of him. So I gave him a kiss. It was only a peck on the lips. I was going to give him a peck on the cheek, but the more I thought about it, the more I thought it needed to be on the lips.

He was so shy about it. We were hugging goodbye and I leaned in and kissed him. His entire body froze. It was cute.

Brandon muttered to himself, "that was my first kiss."

"Well, I hope it was a good one."

That made him look even more confused, like he didn't know if he should thank me or what. I just giggled at him and then Aden made things weird. I swear he thinks he's an action star or a superhero or something.

"We need you to split." Who talks like that? Aden does. He's so lame!

He introduced himself as Nic to Brandon. I don't know why. I guess he thought that Brandon must've known Jad. Maybe I should just call him Nic. I don't like calling him Jad, or even Jaden. The Jad I knew never would've gone two months without shaving. He could've shaved at my place or Lily's at least five times. I get that he couldn't shave while he was in here with the Magicals, but why does he keep walking around like an angry hobo? Does he even care how he looks?

## 67

## Day 1 In The Magical Castle

That was such a wonderful welcome party, Diary! I don't know if you're still up, but I am. It feels so good to be back here! I missed Mama Koko and Captain Alligator and everyone. I don't know if you saw when I gave Princess Platypus the business. Aden isn't even my boyfriend. He never was. I mean, he might've been if Finn hadn't decided to get involved. I can't wait to tell Finn what an assumptive hater he is.

PP tried to act innocent, like, "a Princess would never soil her bill on the flesh of a mortal."

Gimme a fudgy break! PP doesn't even have lust. She just wanted to hurt me. She wanted me to know that she's prettier than me, but she's not. Nobody wants to kiss a fudgy platypus, especially one that sings like a drowning rat! She doesn't even have lips. She kept doing that thing where she turns her bill into heart shaped lips. Kisses don't even look like that! I had to slap her kisses out of the air like five times. What kind of flirting is that? She's about as subtle as her dad.

I can't believe Aden asked for a formal apology from the King and Queen! Why is he complaining? They only threw him on the rack and cut off a limb or too. He's fine now. Aden never could've survived being a Rainbow Warrior. He would've quit after the first month of training.

I hope he'll stop being a pill about the Magicals now that they did apologized. Queen Nephila bowed with all eight of her legs, he's not going to get a better apology then that. I already told him that their gold can't be spent on Earth. When Cap told Aden that we were going to play polo tomorrow, he flipped. I thought he was gonna get himself thrown back into the dungeon. It's a good thing I was there to zip his lips.

Oh, his face was priceless when I did that! When he took his jaw off the table, and asked how I did that, I just zipped my own lips. It feels so good to take Mr. Self-Righteous down a peg. He doesn't want us to stay. Aden didn't even want us to have dinner, but I haven't seen everyone in two months! I miss them!

# 68

## Day 2 In The Magical Castle

I can't believe Cap let me be a team captain! Then again it was my idea to put Aden on Prince Echidna's team; that dandy does little more than play sports all day. He's too skilled for his own good, no one can beat him. We almost did today. I kept goading Aden into coming for me and PE couldn't get at me. It was funny watching them yell at him.

Real talk though, Aden needs to lighten the funk in his diapers. He wouldn't sky race with us because he was too scared of falling off. Even after Cap leapt off the tower and got peeled off the pavement, Aden brought up physics and anatomy and a bunch of other stuff that doesn't matter here. So he stayed behind and "got repeatedly skewered by a manic monotreme." It was just fencing. He's such a drama queen.

It was really good talking to you today, Diary, and I am sorry about how I acted. It's just hard to know what's going on when I'm stuck in lamesville. I didn't know that the Royals were trying to send someone, but Slauson kept the gate closed. My meeting with Stewart Weasel should clear up some of the questions I've been having about the Oath.

I guess I don't need to write you while I'm here, but I've been on Earth so long it's kind of become a habit. Mama Koko finally caught up with me. I hate the taste of soap in my mouth and that wash of lye still stings. She can be such a prude! I am not apologizing for dating Baden or making out with him.

Princess Platypus hasn't given up on Aden. She kept blowing him kisses whether we were playing polo or not. Remember how I told you that I probably shouldn't have left Aden alone to talk to you? That's because she kidnapped him and dragged him over to the gondola to have a romantic boat ride. How romantic could it possibly be if he's tied up and gagged? It's a good thing I was there to save him.

If she knows that he's in love, why does she keep trying to make something happen? I guess sluts are the same in every world. But I'll get back at her tonight. When PP tries to attack Aden in his room, her nasty bug smeared bill is going to land on an Aden dummy. I bet she's already set off the cage trap.

Aden almost didn't go along with my plan. He's being such a pill. I got him a soap box to talk on because he was really laying into me. He was like, "you're so selfish, blah blah blah, if you love the other me why did you kiss Brandon?" So I kissed Brandon goodbye? So what? It was just one kiss. That doesn't mean anything. It's not like we were making out. He doesn't know how to relax and he's got like no imagination.

He kept going on about how we shouldn't be here. It's the Magical Castle! Why wouldn't he want to stay in the Magical Castle? His problem is that he's being too cautious. Remember how he didn't want to sky race? It was like that with everything. Being shot out of a cannon is dangerous. Riding on a dragon is dangerous. Trying to shoot apples off each other's heads is dangerous. Tightrope walking over a volcano is dangerous. This isn't Earth! Nothing is dangerous! What's it going to take for him to get that?

Okay, so the blah blah blah stuff wasn't about Brandon or Baden or me killing myself. He thinks that we're wasting time here when we should be out finding Finn and getting my wand and key back, but we just got here! I'm finally back in the Magical Castle with all my friends and he wants us to leave.

I used to fantasize about taking him here. We'd go on romantic walks in the gardens and slide down rainbows and he'd be so happy. The more he smiled, the more I'd smile, and it would be perfect. But now that he's here, he's just being a boring stick in the mud. No matter what we're doing, he just wants to sit and think of "a way to escape!" We're not prisoners. It's called having a good time. I wish I could think of an activity that would help him flip that switch in his brain and have fun.

Good night, Diary. Hopefully we can talk more tomorrow!

# 69

**Day 3 In The Magical Castle**


I can't believe Sheriff Bulldog dragged me out of bed. King Walrus didn't need to make a big fuss about "imprisoning his daughter," and he definitely didn't need to threaten to decapitate me and Aden. It was just a little prank. She was the one who started it by kidnapping Aden. I kind of feel bad for getting Aden mixed up in that mess. I didn't think he'd pee his pants the second the guards brought their halberds to our necks.

All that pee pee didn't stop PP, did it? She was all water works and fainting spells when we were brought to see the king, but the second we were released and dressed, she was right back to trying to kiss Aden. I don't know what her problem is. I want to go down the moat and see the mermaids, but I don't think Aden will be able to breathe with bubbles. He'll probably bring up water pressure or something stupendously silly.

Do you think I should leave Aden alone again, Diary? I'm just gonna go talk to you.

## 70

## Day 5 In The Magical Castle

You know, as mad as I was when Queen Nephila trapped me in her web, I'm kind of glad she got involved. Being stuck in the Bottle of Sharing really gave Princess Platypus and I a chance to talk.

It wasn't right away, because PP never wants to apologize when she does something wrong. We got into another one of our fights. When I tried to pull off her fake eyelashes, she ripped off my shirt! I took her tiara after that and she finally calmed down. We went to the opposite sides of the bottle and waited for the Queen to let us out. When she finally came around she wouldn't take the cork out, she just gave the bottle a good shake and told us to make up.

Once her mom was gone, and all of the guards had cleared out of PP's room, she actually apologized to me.

"I'm sorry for asking Daddy to execute you."

"He wouldn't have done it."

PP rolled her eyes. "Why do you do that? I'm trying to be nice and you act like you're better than me!"

"That's because I'm a Rainbow Warrior who saved the entire world and you're just a spoiled princess who gets everything she wants! You have no jobs and no responsibilities and contribute absolutely nothing to your father's kingdom!"

"And you do?!"

"I saved the world, that isn't enough for you?"

"It's always the same with you, 'I saved the world, I saved the world!' but you didn't save the world. You couldn't have got out of the pupper strings without Sashy. And Finn is the one who killed Wikella. If saving the world means standing around and doing nothing while your friends fix your mistake, then that must mean that I'm the Queen and the King and the head chef and the most talented wizard in the world! Because all of those people are doing amazing things, and I'm standing next to them while they do it!"

"I didn't make a mistake! I got Wikella to let her guard down! And even if what you're saying is right, when we both know it isn't, I was on other adventures! I fought Wikella and the Troops of Evil 283 times! I didn't get these scars from sitting on a pillow and powdering my face all day!"

"I don't powder my face all day!"

"Whatever."

We were back to pouting. Neither one of us had moved from our side of the bottle. As unpleasant as it was to be in there with her, we weren't going to get out of there if I didn't at least try to patch things up. Besides, PP needed a good spanking since her parents never did it.

"Why can't you just leave Jaden alone? Didn't he tell you that he was in love? Doesn't that mean anything to you?"

"He was lying."

"What do you mean he's lying? You don't have a lie detector. You can't read minds, so how can you be so sure?"

"I've seen the way you look at him. You might've convinced yourself that any Jaden is as good as another, but that's the boy that you fell in love with and you haven't gotten over him."

An arrow shot right through my heart, but PP wasn't done.

"But I've also seen how Jaden looks at you and he doesn't love you back. He doesn't even like you. Jaden hates you but you're so entitled that you're probably the only person in your life who doesn't see that."

That was it. I stood up and walked over to yell at her back. "You're wrong! The Jaden in the other world is just like mine and he's loved me for months, maybe even years! He told me about how he fell in love with my spirit, how my imagination and enthusiasm inspired him to keep trying to write what was in his heart instead of what he thought would get the best reaction at club. We're soulmates, Princess Platypus, and a spoiled rich slut like you would never understand what we have!"

"I know that I'll never get to know what love really is. I know that no one will ever love me! I'm doomed to spend eternity sitting at my parent's side, waiting for a marriage that will never come. I don't get to nurse a child or feel a life grow inside me or be with a man who would die for me or want someone so bad that it actually hurts to be apart from them. I know that! Why do you think I'm so jealous of you?"

Princess Platypus was actually crying. It wasn't her usual water works show with a handkerchief and showers that threatened to drown me, she was actually crying.

"PP..."

She turned around and snapped at me. "But at least I know I'll never be loved! You? You had to steal someone's life to feel love and it's not even a love that you earned!"

"I just told you why you're wrong, Jad-"

"Those aren't your accomplishments, Holly! It's just like with how you saved the world! Finn saved the world, not you! He's the one who killed Wikella. He's the one who ended the Troops of Evil! You rode on his coattails and took in his glory but you didn't earn it! You didn't inspire Jad with your enthusiasm for life, the other Holly did! But she couldn't see that in her Jaden's eyes, just like you can't see how much your Jaden hates you!"

Princess Platypus stood up and the full scale of her eight feet in height was imposing and terrifying. Me? I felt like I was three inches tall. Maybe I was.

"You know what disgusts me about you? You can find love. You can go out there and find a man who will love you for who you are but you don't even try. You're obsessed with a teenage boy that you've never had a real conversation with because you were too scared to try!"

"I wasn't scared. I...he's my friend." I was whimpering and

shrinking.

"Is he, Holly? The other Jaden fell in love with that version of you, but this Jaden never did. Why do you think that is?"

I felt like a little girl talking to her. "Where is this coming from, PP? Did you talk to Diary?"

"It's coming from my eyes and brains! From centuries of watching humanity through a tiny little spyglass and seeing them do the same mistakes over and over again. Now stop dodging the question, Holly! Why doesn't Jaden love you?"

"Because I lied to him. But I had to lie. I couldn't tell him the truth about you and this place. If I did, it would've broken the Oath. I can't break the Oath."

"Did the other Holly break the Oath?"

"She told him about you and-"

"Did he believe her? Did he believe that any of this was real?"

"No. It all sounded like make believe to him."

"People always believe what they want to believe. You wanted to believe that you could be a nice normal girl and that Jaden would love you because he'd see something beautiful and special inside of you. But you're not a normal girl. You're a Rainbow Warrior! You never once let yourself be the Rainbow Warrior!"

"How could I? I was trapped! I signed the contract in blood, I took the Oath!"

"We never said that you had to hide your spirit! We never told you to walk around with your head down and not draw attention to yourself! That was you! You didn't show the world who you were and why! Why did you do that?"

"Because I..." I started to cry. I was whimpering and sobbing.

"Why Holly?!"

"I didn't want them to see me. I didn't want them to know how different I was. I wasn't like them. I didn't have their lives. I didn't think like they think! I still don't! I might've been born a human, but I'm not a human anymore. Jaden hates me now because he's seeing me for me. I had to hide who I was because it's too different!" I held myself and cried. "I'm too different."

Princess Platypus cradled me and squeezed me until all the tears were gone. I'd never seen this side of her. She was an immortal child. I didn't know she could be anything more than that. I didn't know she could have feelings like she had and once I did I think it kind of changed things for me. I could talk to her about my pain and she would understand it.

"You're not too different, Holly. You're still a human and there's a human life out there for you. You want to come back here and live with us, but we're stuck, Holly. We're like paintings hung on a wall, no matter how much the frame or the fibers or the oils change, we don't. You already know what it's like to kiss a human boy, do you want to give that up for all time?"

I don't, but I also don't want to give up on living here. I want something like what we have right now. I want to be with Jaden and Lily but I also want to live here. If Aden can come here, why can't I bring everyone else?

I talked to PP about Aden and her. She wants to be with him for real. She wants to have a serious relationship with him, like the kind she's seen humans have. The problem is every time she gets close to him, those feelings turn into something else and she just kind of throws herself at him. I asked her to leave Aden alone and she said that she would.

When the Queen took us out, we thanked her. I'd always hated Princess Platypus growing up. She teased us and played pranks on us and she seemed like this spoiled little girl who got everything she wanted, but maybe that's how she had to act in front of her dad and the court. Maybe she couldn't be herself in the eyes of others.

I tried to have a real talk with Aden under the stars. I told him about how I'd always been lying to him because of the Oath and I admitted that I'd loved him since seventh grade. It was all stuff that he knew, but it felt good to actually tell someone the truth.

"Holly, do you really want to be honest with me?"

"Of course I do!"

"Then tell me why you're keeping us here. Really."

"Ever since you first talked to me about all the cartoons you liked, I wanted to take you here. You liked Avatar and Fairy Tail and I thought, 'I bet he'd love it in the Magical Castle!' But now that you're here you won't even try to have fun."

"Fun? We're here to have fun? They locked me in a cell where I could only eat rats! Is that your idea of fun? I can't grab hammers from out of nowhere. I don't know how to peel myself off the pavement. This world is scary and all of the things here work on a twisted logic that's half childhood cartoon and half nightmare fuel. Maybe if I've been here as long as you have I could figure all of this out, but I'm not going to do that, Holly."

"But why not? We could live here forever! We could wait until humanity comes up with spaceships and time travel and then go back to Earth and try out all the cool technology of the future. Why wouldn't you want to live in a world where no one can ever die?"

"Because I'm not a cartoon, Holly, and neither are you. In order for us to live here, we have to hurt our family and friends. They care about us. I don't want to live here if it means knowing that my mom is crying herself to sleep every night." He held something back. "This world is like a dream, but dreams are only fun because you can wake up and go back to reality. As hard as it is to be alive, I'd rather live and die than turn my back on people that love me. I've seen what your disappearance did to your family. I know what it did to me. I won't do that to them."

"Jaden, can I ask you something about something else?"

He gave a long sigh. "Only if you promise that we're going home tomorrow."

"We are. I promise."

He nodded once, but he still wouldn't look at me. I mean, I get it. The Magical Castle skyline is wonderful, but I still would've liked to have seen his eyes.

"Do you think it's possible to love one person but then still go on to love somebody else? Do you think that people can really move on from a crush when they honestly and truly love that person with all their heart?"

Aden took a long time answering me. I thought he might be blowing me off. I stayed beside him on that balcony and looked out at the sky with him. Each of the stars were bright and vibrant and dwarfed real stars a hundred times over. The meteor showers came in big as comets and they flew across the sky like clouds. The constellations chased each other and fought to pose in the most glorious parts of the sky. It was like watching a TV show but there wasn't any plot and there weren't any consequences.

"I used to think that way about love. I thought that love was a feeling you got when you liked something or when someone did something that made you happy. When I first felt love it was scary. I didn't want to feel that much about someone that wasn't my parents. My parents were always going to be there to love me, but not her. The second I felt that way about her, I knew it wasn't going to work out.

"I told myself not to like her. I squeezed my eyes shut and held my breath and said, 'no! Jaden, find someone else.' I tried to. For a long time I tried to like someone else and for a time I believed that I could. I thought that once we started dating my crush would fade and that I'd stop thinking about her and wishing that I could make her happy.

"If you had asked me that question before you left, I probably would've smiled and nodded with all the confidence of a teacher. 'Of course, Holly. People can always love somebody else.' But I would've been wrong.

"I don't know if people can love again after they've fallen for one person, but I know that you can't make yourself stop loving the person you fell for. But I also think that you can't make yourself love anyone. No matter how right they are for you and no matter how pretty they are, your heart knows what it wants, and it can't be tricked like a machine."

My heart was all butterflies. I couldn't say a thing.

I don't know if he was talking about me, but I know

that I feel that way about him. Not the Jad that's in the other world that's my boyfriend, but this man that was staring at the stars with me. I love him. I love everything about him. He's thoughtful and sweet and he isn't thinking about sex every five seconds because he really cares about what the people in his life are feeling. My Jad was that man. He was always this man, but I left him because I thought he was going to do something with Fifi.

I ruined things with him, Diary. I couldn't stop thinking about how he and Fifi were walking hand in hand. That pain returned to me. Once those memories came back, I couldn't get them out of my head.

"Jaden, what happened with you and Fifi?"

He scoffed and rolled his eyes. "We [f-word], Holly. Is that what you need to hear? If I tell you that Fifi and I bumped uglies can you let go of everything?"

"It's not about that, Jad, I just-"

"Forget it. I'm sorry I snapped at you." He made his way out. "Good night, Holly."

I'm always ruining things like that with him. I hate that we've grown apart. For a couple seconds while we were up on that balcony it really felt like we were going to patch things up, that we could move past everything that happened and be like it was before, maybe even better! Then I had to go and spoil things by asking him about Fifi. I don't care that they've had sex. I just want to know where his heart belongs. I want to know if he still loves me because I know that I still love him. I think I've always known.

## 71

**March 17**

It's always sad leaving the Magical Castle. I can't help but cry when I have to leave my friends behind. It's strange that Princess Platypus is among those friends now, but honestly, she might be my closest friend now. When we hugged goodbye it didn't feel weird. She really wants me to get my wand back and find happiness on Earth. I wish she could have that happiness too. Maybe if I get my wand and Finn's wand, I can collect all of the wands and use them to give Princess Platypus a human body. I think she'd like that. Do you think King Walrus and Queen Nephila would let me do that? She's a good person, she deserves a chance to live a life too.

We're okay by the way. Aden and I are waiting for Aily to come home. I keep thinking of Aden as Jad, as my Jad. He's the man I fell in love with and I can see that now. When his anger cools and he talks to me like a fellow human being, I remember how calm he was. There's this sorrow in his eyes that makes me want to cheer him up. Only I can't do that anymore. He's so different from Baden. I wish I knew what changed Baden.

I've been thinking about what Aden said last night on the balcony. He said that before I disappeared he thought about love in a different way, like it was a feeling or an event. Aden used to think that love was this thing that you could kind of trick yourself into feeling. Which Jaden did Bolly have to deal with before she gave up hope?

So if Aden thought that love was just this feeling that came and went depending on if he was happy, Fifi was the only thing making him happy. She was comforting him and he thought, "she's making me feel good. I must be in love with her."

That makes sense when I think about what Baden said about her. He said that he loved her, but the more time he spent with me, the more he realized that he loved me more. I was special to him. I was always special to him.

It sucks that I know Aden was talking about me last night, but I can't help it. I spent all of this time getting to know Baden. I was always special to him. He loved me before I even killed myself, he's told me that so many times. If Aden never got over that special someone, that means he still loves me, right? It has to!

Ah! I feel like this is getting confusing again, and not just because I don't know if Aden loves me or not, but because I don't want to call him Aden. I should've asked you about this when I had the chance, Diary. I know that how I was explaining things was working, but this is my Jad! He's always been mine.

# 72

When Aily got home, she started crying. She went right to Aden and hugged him tight. They hugged for like over a minute. I had to just stand there and wait for their little reunion to be done. She looks different now. Her hair is longer, but it's kind of messier. She's just wearing it in a really ugly ponytail. I mean, I've seen mourning Lily from world B, but she looks different. More frazzled, but less haunted.

Aily said hello by slapping me.

Like, gee, thanks. Good to see you too.

She hugged me right after the slap and told me. "Don't you ever do something like that to me again."

I apologized. I apologized a lot and my face feels raw from all the crying I did. Aily's really mad at me for disappearing. I thought she wouldn't be that upset because she knew I wasn't really dead, but I guess she had her doubts. We kind of laughed about how I had a black eye from one Aily and a swollen cheek from the other.

Aden made me tell Aily why I took off.

She didn't get mad. She didn't really say anything, she just went quiet. I told her about Fifi and Baden and about how Tiff and I were becoming good friends. I also told her about how Bily hated me because she found out that I wasn't the Holly she'd known. I even told her about how Baden had cheated on me with Fifi and how I don't really know if he liked me or if he just wanted us to have sex and she didn't react to any of it. Finally, I just kind of trailed off.

"I got about three hundred and fifty dollars," Aily told us.

"Where'd you get the cash?" Aden asked.

"Allowance mostly. Sometimes I'd tell my mom that I'd want to go to the movies with my friends, but we'd just hang out at Arcadia. I've been skipping lunch too, so that helped. I got a little bit of help from Amber and Rach, not a lot, but enough. They'd mostly give me some food when I was skipping."

I hadn't noticed how much thinner she was from before because Bily was about the same size. Just one more secret my friends had kept from me, I guess.

"I don't understand. Why do we need the money?" I asked them.

"We need to meet up with Finn again. Without that money, we're never going to be able to get to Ohio," Aden explained.

"Wait, so Finn's not here? I thought he came back to open The Gate."

"Holly, that was almost five weeks ago. Aden's been gone for a long time, almost as long as you. What the [h-word] happened?"

"It turns out King Walrus and Queen Nephila are only nice to the Rainbow Warriors. Every other human that enters their realm is immediately met with suspicion. After that, they held me until Holly's backup boyfriend was able to take down the cameras around the gate."

"Brandon isn't a backup boyfriend! I don't even like him like that. You're making me sound like a slut."

"Holly, I don't give a [s-word] about your love life." There was no warmth in Bily's voice. None at all. It wasn't a joke, she just didn't want to hear about it. Unlike Aden, she didn't even want to bring it up to tease me.

She went on. "You and Jaden will go to Ohio and convince Finn to lend you his wand. Once you get back, Holly can get the wand and key and we can be done with this mess, right?"

"I might have to go with her to the other world," Aden said. "In order to get out of the dungeon, I had to agree to take a quest to return her wand and key to the Magical Castle."

"You can't do that. Those are my items!"

"Then take them back with me, Holly. I made an agreement with those psycho cartoons, and I am not going to go back on it!"

"Cartoons?"

"The Magicals are cartoons, Lily. They're like three to fifteen feet tall and have no concept of right or wrong. I don't know what you did, Lily, but the fact that you can't go through The Gate doesn't mean you're a bad person. Trust me."

She just dropped her head. I had a pretty good idea what she'd done and it was a bad thing. High schoolers shouldn't be messing around with men in college.

I raised my hand and Aden called on me. "Look, that's a good plan and all, but it's not going to work. Finn has to come with us. Each of the Rainbow Wands are bonded to one person. I can't use the Ruby Wand just like Detective Slauson can't use the Emerald Wand. I need to call him and from there we should be able to send him the money to get a bus ride here."

"We tried to get Finn to come with us the first time," Aily explained. "He wouldn't go. He said that the Magicals would be mad at him."

"Besides, he said he dropped the wand in the bottom of the ocean," Aden reminded me.

"He's lying. He's been lying about everything. I don't think we can believe anything Finn said. He has the wand, I'm sure of it. He might've burned his Diaries and gave you his key, but he wouldn't get rid of the wand, they're too powerful to just toss down the ocean. It would find a way back to him. Let me worry about talking to Finn. I'll convince him to come."

Even though Aily and Aden don't like me anymore, they at least seemed to trust me. At least they trusted me when it came to all this magic stuff.

Aily handed me her phone.

"What?"

"You said you were going to call him."

"I didn't think I needed to do it now!"

Aden spoke up. "Holly, I've been gone for over a month. I told my parents I'd be gone for a few days. They probably think I'm dead. I don't want to draw this out."

"They don't think he's dead, right Lily?"

She shook her head. "He's been declared dead. I had to lie to the police. I was at his funeral."

That killed the mood.

Aily wiped her eyes and Aden followed her out of the room. When I tried to go too, Aden told me to make the call and shut the door. Looks like they're both really mad at me. But we've had fights before. Now that everything's out in the open, they'll come around.

Here's how the super intense phone call went:

"Lily, is there something new? Are they back?"

"Hello, Finn."

"Holly."

"Yeah, Holly. Still taking antipsychotics to deal with a childhood of lies."

Finn chuckled. "Mad at me for that, are we?"

"You're goodly gosh right I am!"

"You're still following the Oath." He sighed.

"Of course I am! How else could I have come back from the other world?"

"What do you need?"

"I need your help."

"With?"

"I lost my wand and key. I hid them under a rock and a detective found it; a gun toting police officer. I need you to come back to the other world take it from him!"

"I don't think you know what you're asking me to do, Holly."

"I don't care, Finn! I don't care if seeing King Walrus and Queen Nephila gives you a panic attack or whatever! You lied to me for years. You planted seeds in my head that the Oath and the Rainbow Warriors and all of it was nothing but lies! We were supposed to be friends forever and you abandoned Sashy and me! You owe me, Finn."

He let out a long sigh. "Fine. I'll be there tomorrow."

"Okay, we'll send you some money and...wait, what do you mean tomorrow?"

"I'll explain when I see you, Holly. I promise you, this time I'll tell you the truth; all of it. Are you going to be at Lily's house?"

"There or by The Gate."

"Okay. It's good to hear your voice, Holly. I'm sure your friends are happy you're back."

"Oh, they're just thrilled."

And then he hung up! Good to know the new honest Finn is busy chowing down jerk chicken.

He sounded worse than before. Before Finn sounded like he was a Christian trying to save my soul. Now he sounds like Thanatos. What did he mean about the whole truth? Do you know what Finn's talking about, Diary? Has he been keeping things from me since before he started "seeing a therapist?"

Lily's done with homework. She wants to turn the lights out. Well, it's just gonna be a night with the three of us sleeping in one room and I can't use the bathroom. This should be a piece of cake, right?

# 73

**March 18**

We still got another hour until Finn arrives. I don't know why he thinks he knows more than me. I'm the one who stayed close to the Magicals, while he's been ignoring them. It's kind of like Rude Boy to pull something like this. One more stunt, one last prank before he helps me get my wand and key back. On the phone he made it sound like I didn't have a clue about what was really going on.

I went on a walk with Aily early on. After the night we had, I was glad to get out of here. I don't think I slept for more than thirty minutes. She wanted to talk about lies and trust. She'd never known that I was keeping something that big from her. As Aily put it, there was no way that she could've figured out that I was a childhood superhero, but she should've at least put together that I was keeping something big from her.

"I always thought there was some trauma with your friends, but never something like this. How can I trust you after this? You're clearly an accomplished liar."

"I didn't have a choice, Lily. I never did any of this to hurt you."

"I know. I want to trust you, Holly. I want to forgive you for what you did, but I don't know how. How could you just leave us like that?"

It was a hard question to answer. I knew from talking to Bily, World B Lily, that there was a good chance that things could turn into a big fight where we're both screaming at each other. There had to be some way to tilt the truth to make her understand where I'm coming from. Some lie that satisfied her outrage. She basically told me that she couldn't tell a truth from a lie, so I didn't need to tell the truth.

But that was kind of the point, wasn't it? Aily had suffered because I didn't care enough about them to stick around. Now that I could be honest, shouldn't I? If we were going to be friends after this, she needed to know the truth. So I told her.

"I gave up on Earth a long time ago, Lily.

"I was eleven when I first thought about going to the Magical Castle and never coming back. We'd found another one of Wikella's strongholds. Most of her lairs were sinister, gloomy, and a fight from the moment we stepped inside. This place was different. It looked normal, like a really big house that people get married in. But it felt wrong. The walls looked like there were ants moving just under the paint, the carpet would squeak and bleed when we stepped on it, and the whole place smelled like spoiled meat.

"The monsters were coming from the bedrooms. We usually fought dumb aggressive monsters like ogres, snapdragons, banshees, and spider ladies. That was the first time we met what we called Brains. Their heads were about twice as large as they should be, and their heads would wobble and shake when they moved. We could hear them crying and yipping at the walls. They scratched at their bodies like people and they fought to occupy the same space. When they came at us they attacked with coordination, yelling wordless orders at each other to regroup and probe for weaknesses.

"Before then, we'd always been able to beat the smaller monsters without using our special attacks. Our regular attacks were missing. We were freaking out and running scared. Finally, Finn went aggro and lit the whole place on fire. Something about the sight of burning walls spurred us to action. We regrouped and took them out.

"The Brains were gone, but we still needed to get the Twisted. It wasn't even the scariest thing we'd seen by that point, he was just a beetle with his own head. He made the monsters by laying eggs, but he was fast and he could break through our armor. That was the first Twisted we'd met that could do that. All of our old tricks were useless on him.

"Sasha saved us. She'd already used her special and her water attacks weren't doing anything to him anyway. So she used herself as bait. She just ran out into the middle of the room and threw her arms out. He pinned her down to sting her and that gave us the opening to work out a combined special. We had to use three at once to take down the beetle bane.

"Wikella couldn't make evil. All of her generals and scientists were once Magicals who'd turned their backs to serve her. The rest of her Troops of Evil came from people. She'd find bullies or kids without any friends and bring out the wickedness inside. Their anger, fear, and spite would get worse and worse until the Rip, a moment where the person lost touch with civilization and acted for themself. That's what made them go from a pupper to a Twisted.

"Sometimes we were able to find kids who were still puppers and extract Wikella's magic before they transformed, but once they were Twisted, we needed to enter their minds and find some way to save them. If we didn't, then the magic would linger inside and they'd Rip again. Once we killed the Twisted, the monsters would disappear along with all of their corruption. We'd see what the place was like without Wikella's magic.

"That house was basically the same. It was a fancy house that looked like it was used to host parties. The lair was almost a perfect reflection of the real world. It was somehow scarier that way. The reason the place and the monsters were so unimaginative but horrifying, was because Wikella had found a way to corrupt adults. She'd always used her magic on kids because their minds were malleable, they could believe in magic. This was a man who accepted magic, because he wasn't well.

"His Rip wasn't yelling at his parents, breaking all of his toys, or setting his house on fire. This man had killed and raped a woman. One moment we're combining our specials to kill a creepy bug monster and the next we're standing above a man and a naked corpse. Nothing could've prepared us for that sight. Some of us puked, some of us left the room. I stayed. I knew that the worst was yet to come, because we'd have to go into this man's mind and help him get better.

"It was just going to be me, Finn, and Blake going inside, but Sasha insisted on going with us. She was the leader and if Wikella was corrupting adults, she figured that she needed to understand how.

"This man was deeply disturbed. He was teased growing up because he was quick to cry. We'd helped kids like that before, their intense emotions made their monsters stronger, but their emotional center ultimately made it easier to help them get past that. It was far too late for something like that with him. By middle school, he'd turned into an outcast who fantasized about killing his classmates. By high school, he'd focused his hatred on women. His first sexual experience was with a woman too drunk to even wake up. He only turned into a sexual predator after that.

"As sick as his mind was, we kept looking. Sasha kept us focused, urging us to look for benchmarks and emotional tethers that could make this man remember civilization and the value of working with others. Then we found the court trials and the meetings with police officers. We saw him enter the system and leave on early parole. We saw him rape a fifteen-year-old girl and get released to rape another.

"I left. The others followed. They gathered around me. Everyone was talking, trying to convince me to collect myself to go back inside. We had to find some core of humanity to bring him back. Finn, Blake, and Sasha knew we had to finish our job. We couldn't subject that filth to our friends. It was too late for us, but they were still safe in thinking that this man had only committed murder at his Rip. They tried to talk me into going back in, but Finn didn't.

"We locked eyes and knew what needed to be done. I learned that day that we could use our powers in the real world. I learned that the same spikes and energy blasts that fried ogres could easily break apart a human skull. I did what society and the law didn't do because it was too civil to do. I killed that man."

I waited a long time for Aily to say something. It was a lot to take in, even without all of the magical stuff that probably confused her. I'd shared my first kill. She could probably put together what happened next. Wikella gave up on finding kids who might've become killers one day and upgraded to corrupting rapists, murderers, drug addicts, and other criminals so deranged that reality was a subjective decision they accepted one day at a time. We developed the rule of three. Three heinous crimes and their lives were forfeit.

When Aily didn't say anything, I continued. "It wasn't just that there were bad people. We'd seen the lives of too many kids to believe that people were basically good. No, it was the apathy and impotence of the law that took away my faith. I could live a perfect life. I could be good and kind and decent and then some unhinged monster could take everything away from me.

"Growing up wasn't something I looked forward to. It wasn't even something that I wanted to happen. I gave up on growing up. I gave up on being a human. I slept at the Magical Castle that night. The others came back to talk me out of living there. I wouldn't go back and eventually they had to leave me there. It was Mama Koko who helped me. She's a wise old gorilla in a bonnet. She told me that there were parts of life that I couldn't feel in the Magical Castle. That life had things to offer me, good things. She convinced me to try living on Earth until I had every experience I could. If I still wanted to live in the Magical Castle, no one would stop me.

"So that's what I've been doing. Every time I eat new food, every time I have fun with you or my friends, I ask myself the question, 'is this enough?' Is this enough of a reason to stay on Earth?

"Before I went to the other world, my answer was always, 'no.' It isn't enough. There's only misery and heartbreak for me here, and that's assuming that I live a normal life."

"So you gave up on living." Aily was mad. Mad as she was when she punched me in the face in the other world.

"I didn't give up on living, I just gave up on Earth."

"That's great for you, but what's everyone else supposed to do? What about me? If you were me would you just take your life? Sure there's evil out there, but there's good too, Holly. Some people live their entire lives without ever seeing the kind of evil you're talking about!"

"Not from my experience. Every mind I've ever entered, every life I've ever lived as a spectator has been one of pain, fear, hatred, and constant disappointment."

"Yeah, because you were living the lives of psychopaths! You entered the minds of people that some magical evil witch had targeted. That's not a fair view of humanity. Haven't you ever considered the fact that a person who was basically good couldn't be corrupted by Wikella?"

"I used to, but I realized that was just wishful thinking."

"How can you say that? How can you be so certain that this witch, Wikella, didn't just target the worst of mankind?"

"She targeted children. For almost three years we fought other children, kids like us that were just having a bad week, or going through their parent's divorce. The smallest little things were enough for them to curse at their parents or push their siblings down stairs or throw their pets across the room. Kids are supposed to be the best of us, the innocent minds uncorrupted by a life of evil. But even if that wasn't true and Wikella somehow managed to only find the wicked children, I know that humanity is susceptible to corruption!"

"How?!"

"Because she got to me, Lily! She reached inside my mind and made me a pupper. It didn't feel different. I didn't lose control of my body or lose the ability to feel the world around me. All it took was a simple change in my perspective. I knew that my actions weren't important. I knew that no one really cared about anything I did and I was able to let go of it all.

"After the Rainbow Warriors helped me, I wasn't a bad person. I could still walk through The Gate. I was still a good person. That could only have been possible if I was a good person before I was corrupted."

"But Holly, I couldn't go into The Gate. Do you honestly think that I'm a bad person?!"

I didn't want to say it. I knew what she was capable of. I knew why she wasn't let in, and I think she saw that in my eyes.

"What? What have I done that's so horrible?"

"Tell me about your violin teacher."

Aily looked away.

"I know what you did, Lily. I know what you did because the other you did it too. She's been having sex with him for almost three months. She keeps telling me that things are over, and that's how I know the last time wasn't the last time. She keeps lying to herself, but she-"

She told me to be quiet. "I didn't have sex with him!"

I couldn't tell if Aily was lying. She sounded sincere and she even looked it.

Here's the story that Aily told me. "Before you left I tried to, okay? I tried to make something happen, but it didn't work. He treated me like a little girl and cancelled our sessions. I haven't seen him since."

"You kissed him?" I don't know why I pried, I guess I had to know how similar she was to Bily. I still don't understand why the other world is so different.

"I tried to. I got close to him, I put my hand on his crotch, and moved in for a kiss. He stopped me before our lips touched, he grabbed my hands, and then he sat me down and told me that he couldn't teach me anymore. It was one of the most embarrassing things I'd ever done. I'm not the other Lily, but even if I was, even if I was sleeping with my violin teacher, do you honestly think that makes me a bad person?"

"It doesn't matter," I admitted. "The Magicals think that's enough, so you can't go there."

"Why does it matter so much to you if I can go into the Magical Castle? From everything Jad tells me, it sounds like a nightmare!"

"It's a paradise. We're just too used to living in hell to appreciate a good thing."

"I don't think that's true, Holly."

I should've stayed quiet, but I was in full honesty mode and I didn't want to give it up. "I wanted you to come with me. You're my best friend, Lily. I love you. I wanted you and Jad to come with me to the Magical Castle so we could be there for all time. Now that you can't, I don't know what I'm going to do. I don't think Jad would come anyway and-"

"Holly, stop. You're not a Magical."

"I know that."

"You can't live in the Magical Castle. You can't just turn your back on humanity and life. I know that there's a lot of evil in this world, but it's all you can see. If you're only here to have a good experience, what are you supposed to do when all of the bad moments come? What happens to you when you have a bad day, do you just think to yourself, 'maybe it's time to leave Earth?'"

"Kind of. It's more like...I don't like how you're talking to me. You're making it seem like my plan is a bad thing, but shouldn't I try to be happy? If you could live a life without pain where you never have to work, wouldn't you?"

"No!"

"Seriously, Lily?!"

She rolled her eyes and seethed. "It's a dumb question!"

"No, it isn't! It's a very simple question! You can live in paradise or you can live here, which are you going to pick?"

"That's not a question that people should have to answer, not really. I'm not you! I can't go to some magic world where cartoons are your friends and most people can't! We don't have the choice to go to a world where we can never die."

"Right, so since I can, that means I should."

"No, because it's not...natural. It's not human. Don't you get it? What you've been through, the things that have happened to you, they keep you from learning how to grow up and cope with all of the bad [s-word]."

I almost slapped her. It would've served her right if I did. "I am not immature!"

"You want to go to a magic world where your friends are all giant cartoons. What part of that sounds mature? You're not learning how to deal with problems, you're analyzing life like it's a [d-word] math equation! If your life is bad you'll go through The Gate, if it's good, you'll stay. We don't have that option!"

"I saved the world! I killed people so you wouldn't get ripped apart by monsters or eaten alive!" I was so mad that I was crying.

"So what? Because you did a good thing the normal rules shouldn't apply to you?"

"Yes! No. There aren't any rules. What you're talking about isn't a thing. People don't have to live here."

"Why, because they can kill themselves?"

"Yes!"

Lily was quiet. It wasn't a seething quiet or one born out of confusion. She was worried about me. Maybe it wasn't even worry. She looked at me like she was seeing me for the first time in her life.

"I didn't mean that. I'm not saying that you should kill yourself. I'm not saying that anyone should kill themselves. It's just...I don't know why you're acting like I'm insane because I want to go off to live in the Magical Castle. When Frodo destroyed the ring, he got to sail off with the elves and live happily ever after. Sam didn't give him a big speech about how he was being crazy and selfish, but every single time I try to collect a reward, that's all I get. It doesn't matter if it's you, or Jaden, or fu...fudgy Princess Platypus, everyone gives me a hard time for wanting my happily ever after."

"Holly, I want you to promise me something."

"I don't know if I can. I have to know what it is before I make a promise. When I make a promise I keep it."

Lily took my hands. She had this condescending look in her eyes. "I want you to promise that you'll give the wand and key to the Magicals and come back here. I want you to come back to your parents and live a normal life without an escape button. If you do, I promise you that things will be different. They'll feel different."

I shook my head so hard tears were flying off my cheeks. "They won't."

"They will. You don't know how different things will be because it's a life that you never lived. If you come back..." Lily let out a long sigh. "Please think about it, okay?"

I nodded. "I don't think you're a bad person, Lily."

She let go of my hands.

"Lily."

"Just think about what I said, okay?" She walked into her house, our little walk done.

Aden and Aily haven't been in to check on me. They're content to let me sit in here and write about everything that happened. We're not friends anymore. Why should I come back to a world where I have no friends and no one loves me?

# 74

Diary!

Finn's been lying to us! He's been lying to all of us for years! Wikella is with him! She's alive! If you've been waiting for a reason to talk to King Walrus and Queen Nephila, this is it! Send everyone you got through the gate. I know we don't have the Rainbow Warriors, but if you send a surprise attack, you could probably overwhelm her. She's just standing outside Aily's house talking to Aily, Aden, and Finn. You have to send someone, please! This doesn't make any sense.

I told Finn that I need to think. You can use this time to send someone to kill him and Wikella. This is it. We can still stop her and save the world for real this time.

Finn says that he teleported here. He says that the wands have way more power than we were ever told about; that we don't even need the Magical Castle. According to Finn, the Magical Castle and all the Magicals were made by the wands, but that can't be right, can it? It's just another one of his lies. I can't believe anything he says.

It's Wikella though. It's definitely Wikella. I'd recognize that smile anywhere. I can't believe she's just walking around with a hoodie jacket on. She's a cartoon with pale white, actually white, skin! People must've seen her walking around with normal clothes. You can't walk around everywhere with gloves without raising some eyebrows.

Finn faked Wikella's death with an illusion, maybe that's what's really going on. She could be an illusion. That could explain some things, but not everything. How can he do an illusion without being transformed? How can he even do an illusion in the first place? That was Liv's power. Even if he got the Topaz Wand, he couldn't use it.

What's going on, Diary? I need answers.

He says if he goes through the gate, he's going to have to take over the Magical Castle. He couldn't do that, right? General Leo and Admiral Orca would destroy him! They need to ready their forces. You need to act, Diary. Send the armies out. Why aren't you sending them?

You can't just be another mirror, Diary. You have to be real. Do something to prove that you're real.

PLEASE!

## 75

Finn walked up to the house with Wikella. We saw them coming from Lily's parent's room, so we all went down to meet him. He asked for me to swear parlay, and I did. I thought he was worried that I would attack him, but once I swore to parlay, that witch took off her hood.

Wikella.

She was just as pale and wicked as I remembered, with eyes that glowed like coals on the darkest night, and lips of stars on ebony. Her skin a sickly white, her hair was long and shone like a raven's feather. Seeing her made me grab for my wand, but I only found my secret markers. I got between her and my friend, threw my arms out, and told them to run.

She laughed.

"It's nice to see you too, Holly. You and your friends aren't in any danger."

"Quiet! Your lies won't work on me!"

Finn spoke up. "She's not lying, Holly. We're not here to hurt you and even if we were, what could you do?" He held up his wand. I could see the shine of the ruby. He didn't need to make a bigger threat than that. Transformed, he could burn the entire neighborhood down if he wanted to.

"You're bluffing. You betrayed the Magicals! You broke the Oath and everything that we stood for, you can't-"

He spoke the words, "radiant ruby."

I covered my eyes but I could still see the flash of light and feel the heat of the flames as they burned away his clothes to reveal a teenager wearing the sparkling outfit of the Ruby Warrior. He'd changed. He spared Wikella's life, broken the Oath, betrayed everything the Rainbow Warriors stood for, and was still able to transform. With a snap and a puff of smoke he was back to being a stuck up sixteen-year-old in generic Target wear.

"Can we cease the theatrics?" he asked like I was flipping out for no reason. "Where should we start?"

"You could start by taking a long walk into a black hole!" I told him. I tried to get Aily and Aden to run, but Aden actually walked around me.

"You're Wikella."

She bowed. "One and the same. I used to be the Queen of All Evil, but I've been..." she paused to smirk. Oh, how I hate her! "'Rebranding' since then. My priorities have changed, my anger has eased, and now I'm the vision of unearthly beauty you see before you."

"How can you be in this world? I thought cartoons..." Aden shook his head. "I thought Magical couldn't leave."

"Did they tell you that?" Wikella asked him. After he nodded she looked to me. "Would you be a dear and tell them the truth, Holly?"

I ground my teeth.

Finn answered him. "They can pass through The Gate, but it changes them. That's how we were recruited in the first place. Caretaker Mole passed through the gate and invited us to go to the other side. It bled his color, rounded out his features, and slowly turned him into something more human. Eventually it killed him. He died to get us to follow him into The Gate and take the Oath to become Rainbow Warriors."

"So how come you're alive?" Aden asked of Wikella.

I answered before Wikella and Finn could lie about her origin. "Because she's been feeding off the souls of the living! Wikella found a way to turn human beings into pure magic; consumption!"

"That's how it started," Wikella admitted. She didn't sound all that contrite about it either. "Feasting on humans, while effective, was largely unsustainable. My first feedings were gruesome and sloppy. I devoured a person neck to navel, but I learned. I learned that I could survive by only eating the human heart and eventually I was able to survive with little more than a trickle of blood."

I couldn't take it. I snapped at them. "Finn, you traitor! How can you stand there and listen to her talk about killing people?!"

Finn gave a half shrug. "It's in the past, Holly. Our hands are hardly clean."

"We killed people because we had to! Those people were murderers and rapists!"

"I had too as well," Wikella spoke again. "I did what I did because I didn't have a choice, Little Emerald. Any creature that hungers will eat. Humans don't care about the feelings or the soul of a cheeseburger."

Aden kept talking to her like she was a person. I don't think he understood how evil she really was. "Okay, so you were this evil vampire witch thing, I get that, but how did you become this Queen of All Evil. Why would you even call yourself that?"

Wikella tilted her head to find the words. "I had a different way of thinking than humans did."

Finn jumped in to fill the holes. "It's because of where she came from. The Magicals believed in absolute good and absolute evil. Her mind wasn't capable of considering the possibility of simply being a thing that existed. Since she wasn't good, she had to be evil. That part of her was starting to break down, but the more she interacted with human media and propaganda, the more she came to believe that she was an agent of evil. She even thought she was a messenger of Satan."

"Those were troubled times, for sure." Wikella gave a little chuckle at her ignorance.

Aden was still all about talking to her and trying to find what her deal was. "So what changed?"

"Growth. As I fed from humans, I learned that magic had to be connected to the human soul. While drinking from a resting vile of blood gave me no sustenance, other actions did."

Aden looked to me.

"Torture. She learned that she could gain magic from strapping people up and poking them. She literally fed off their fear. Wikella made a castle in our world and filled a dungeon with people to torture and feed from. When the Magicals found out that she was still alive, they sent others to capture her and bring her in, but she corrupted them all."

"Don't be so reductive, Holly. They were corrupted by the time they found me, they had no choice. Living in this world is a drain. Being here is like living in a world without gravity, where every pump of your heart must be pounded by your own hand. They were little more than beasts when I found them. With my help, they could survive in your world."

"Enough with the exposition!" I snapped. "What do you want, Wikella? Why are you here?!"

"Why, we're here to help you, Holly." She looked to Finn.

"You asked for my help and I thought you were owed some answers. This isn't some big villain monologue. I came here as your friend."

I was sick of this. He wasn't a good guy and Finn definitely wasn't my friend! "But why should I believe anything that you said?! You know what she is! Every day she lives on Earth she brings nothing but pain and misery!"

"That's not true." Finn walked up and took her hand. They interlaced their fingers. "While she does need the magic of the human soul, fear isn't the only way to get it."

"She's feeding off your love," Aily gasped.

Wikella nodded. "Sometimes it can be from a small gesture of affection, sometimes I can feel the magic from a kind smile or the rage of people ranting at me over inane things."

"She spends a lot of time online," Finn chuckled.

"Are you fu...are you frick frackin kidding me?! You betrayed us all so you could date her?!"

"It makes you mad enough to swear, does it?" Wikella arched a brow.

"You don't need to do that [s-word]," said Finn. "Swearing, curse words, all of the rules don't matter, Holly."

"We swore an Oath to the Royals!"

"Right, we took an oath, but how is that oath reinforced? The Magicals can't read our minds and they don't know everything we do. Good and evil are concepts in the human mind, how can they possibly know what's good and what isn't?"

"But The Gate!"

Finn smiled. "See, The Gate is actually how I figured out that the Oath was meaningless. At first, I thought that angels must've been the ones checking our souls, but it didn't make any sense. Blake was Jewish. If he believed in one God and I believed in another, how could we both be good? As the years went by I devised test for goodness. Every single one failed to differentiate between us. One of us might be good by one standard, but never all. Then you killed someone.

"That should've been it. That should've been the road of no return. When you crushed that man's skull I thought you were giving it all up. You gave up the power, the responsibility, all of it, but you were able to go back through The Gate like it wasn't even a big deal. You even returned to hide."

Aden whispered to me, "you killed someone?"

"Later."

"See The Gate can't measure morality. The Gate only ever did one thing, it checked for guilt. We weren't chosen because we were good kids, we were chosen because we were all selfish or short-sighted enough to not carry around blame. The same thing was true for swearing and the Oath. Why was 'idiot' okay but '[s-word]' was banned? They mean the same thing. There's no such thing as good and evil, Holly. There never was."

"That sounds exactly like what a supervillain would say!"

Finn rolled his eyes.

"Okay, so if you're really going to help Holly, then why did Wikella come?" Aily asked.

"I can go through The Gate no problem, but once I do, they're going to attack. They didn't figure it out when it first happened, but it's been five years." He held up a hand full of wands, every color but mine.

"Have you lost your mind! If she gets those-!"

Aden got in my way to push me back. "Holly, they can still kill you."

"I'm not a servant of evil anymore, Holly. I haven't so much as cut anyone in years. I don't have urges to commit evil. I don't even get mad, I never have. I thought that I was making the world a better place, I thought it was my role to reshape the Earth. I don't care about any of that anymore. I just..." Wikella looked back to Finn with an approximation of love in her eyes.

"She wants to be human, Holly. She wants to live a human life and die. If I can borrow your wand, I can change Wikella. We..." The traitor grabbed her hand again. "We want to be a family. We've been waiting four years for you to give up on Earth and run away to the Magical Castle or a different reality. You can still have that Holly, but we can't get to the other world without confronting the Royals."

"We don't have to do this though, Holly," Wikella assured me. "Finn and I can keep waiting. We were thinking about waiting until he's 18 anyway. If you don't think it's worth breaking up the Magical Castle, we'll stay here. You're smart, Holly, you can-"

"No! Fudge you! Fudge you and your fudge covered nuts! Do not compliment me! Don't even think about it. In fact, don't even talk to me! I'm not going to lead you to the Magical Castle and watch you destroy them!"

"I don't understand, Finn," Aily spoke up. "If you and Wikella could've destroyed the Magical Castle at any point in time, why haven't you?"

"We have no reason to. They exist in their realm, and we're safe where we are. Wikella doesn't want to go back and neither do I."

"I'm going back to the house!" I stormed off.

"Holly, wait."

"I need to think!"

My own personal Benedict Arnold called out to me. "Diary won't work. It's not real. That cartoon flying book is just a fancy mirror. It can't tell you anything that you haven't thought yourself and it doesn't talk to the Royals. You can't warn them that we're coming, Holly."

And that's how we got here.

I don't know what to think anymore. I feel so tired, but I need to make a decision. I can't put the Magical Castle in danger just to get my stuff back. There has to be a way out of this. There has to be!

# 76

Dear Diary,

I never liked that phrase because it felt like I was any other girl writing to myself, but then that's what it's always been. I was talking to myself the whole time. The Royals used magic to create a cartoon floating book that talked back to me and I never realized it.

You're not real, Diary. I've had conversations with you about what I should do and how I should act and you always had an answer. Maybe I should've known you weren't alive when you always came up with an idea I was already considering. Real friends always disagree about something, but you never did.

Am I just writing to myself now? I guess I always have been. How did Finn figure out the diaries weren't real? He seems to know so much about the wands and the magic. If I'm going to kill him, I need a good trap. He'll know something's up the second I try to take his wand. If I could transform, I might be able to beat him in a solo fight.

No. I know in my heart that Finn would be ready for that. I thought Wikella was dead. I believed that we'd conquered evil and stopped training. From the sound of things, Finn is stronger than he was in sixth grade. At my peak, I would've struggled to take Finn down. He and I were always the best fighters, but now it wouldn't even be a contest. I have to kill him with trickery.

Things aren't all bad. He's pretending to be one of the good guys still. King Walrus and Queen Nephila wanted to hold a parade to honor his return, but we politely refused. I might be able to use the noise and spectacle to distract him. During the festivities I could jam a knife in his throat. Things would be a lot easier if I had a gun.

No, killing Finn is definitely possible, I just have to learn his weakness. He trusts me enough to leave Wikella behind and try doing it my way, but he wouldn't do that if he didn't think he could take on the entire Magical Army by himself. He can't be that powerful, can he?

Aily still couldn't use The Gate. She's gotta be with Wikella still. If I kill Finn at the Magical Castle, she's going to know something's up when we come out without him. But does it really matter? If I kill Finn I'll have all seven of the wands. Maybe there's some way to combine the powers and destroy Wikella once and for all.

Another way to stop them would be to wait for Finn to transform Wikella to a human, but that's gotta be a trap. Once he gets my wand, they've won. The only risk is to Aden and Aily. They're being used as hostages. Finn is with Aden and Aily is waiting behind with Wikella. I can still beat them. I need a weapon and an opportunity.

# 77

**Another Day. I Don't Know When.**


Aden was walking out in the gardens. He said he was thinking. I can't blame him. It's such a beautiful place. The ponds are full of frogs, koi, and starfish of every color. The roads are decorated with mosaics of the royals and the history of magic. Every bush and petal is cultivated like a living painting. And of course there's that gorgeous night sky that we'll never have on Earth. Spending time in the gardens, it's easy to let your thoughts wander.

"Lily asked me to come back to your world."

"You told her that you couldn't come back," Aden guessed.

"I told her I'd think about it."

He grunted. What is that? Do men think we know what they're saying when they just grunt? How hard is it to use words? He knew what I wanted from him, but no he can't make it that easy. Once we get back to World B everything is going to happen fast. I needed to talk to Aden right then and there.

"I still love you, Jad."

He sounded mad. "No, you don't. I don't know if you ever loved me."

"But I do!" I tried to get in front of him so I could look into his eyes but he wouldn't look at me. "How can you say that, Jad? I went to another world to be with you. I left my family and friends so that we could be together!"

"I was one of those friends, Holly. I thought you were dead! Do you have any idea what that's like?"

"Of course, I do! The Rainbow Warriors were my friends. I had to watch four of them die and I had to see more of the Magicals die too. I know what it's like to lose someone!"

"Then why would you subject me to that? How could you bring me that pain, if you honestly and truly loved me?"

"But it isn't that simple, Jad!"

"It is. All of this stuff about magic and Wikella and alternate worlds doesn't change the fact that you intentionally hurt everyone you love just to have your perfect life!"

I tried to grab his hands but Aden used the railing to keep me at bay. "You're a huge part of that perfect life, Jad! Lily doesn't love me. In both worlds, she hates me. She's turned her back on me and our friendship so many times, even before I disappeared. And my parents? They barely knew I was alive! All they cared about was their jobs and their affairs and finding the perfect cocktail of alcohol and opioids to stop giving a shady coin. Everyone else at school couldn't pick me out of a lineup."

"You're wrong!"

"I'm not! I didn't have an impact there, I didn't matter!"

"Then why is the other world so different? You keep talking about how I've changed and how you're not even sure if the other Jaden is like me. Why is that, Holly? Why would Lily and I be so different in that world?"

"Because I killed myself, I know."

"It's not just that. We're different because you were different, Holly. You didn't have the weight of humanity on your shoulders. You didn't watch your friends die off one by one while you fought a war with an immortal vampire witch. You never had to kill people and tell your friends so many lies that you could barely keep them straight. That Lily and the other me are different because you had an impact on their lives, just like you had an impact on my life."

"Oh, Jad!" I reached for him, but again he dodged me. "You impacted my life too. I love you, can't you see that? I never stopped loving you."

"You mean even as you were [f-word] my doppelganger?"

"You can't be jealous, Jad, and we've never had sex. I wasn't seeing anyone else, I was dating you!"

"By hurting me! You hurt me to date me! You hurt every

single person you knew to have a relationship with me. What part of that sounds like love? Since you can't seem to get this into your head, lemme make something perfectly clear: I never loved you. That other Jad might've, I don't know. From everything you've told me about him, he kind of sounds like a selfish prick.

"All I know is what I feel. I don't love you and I was never even sure if I could be your friend. You were always guarded around me, and that armor never came off. I tried so hard to get you to open up about your pain and all it ever did was make you come up with another lie, a lie that you refused to back down from. On paper, we were good for each other. You liked to write, you had big thoughts about humanity and people, and I was always attracted to you, but it never turned into anything more than that.

"You say that you loved me, but you couldn't have. You didn't know who I was. The more you kept from me, the more I kept from you. I never talked to you about how miserable my parents made me. I never told you about the novel I started, because I didn't show it to anyone. I never told you about my friends trying to convince me that you were too damaged to spend time with or how I felt like everyone in my life was pushing me to be with Fifi."

"You didn't need to." I reached for Aden's face and this time he let me touch him. "And not because I went into your dreams or used the mirror to see what the other versions of you were like. I didn't do that. I never used magic to trick you into loving me. I knew what you were going through because of who you were. I was always watching you, Jad. I knew Fifi was wrong for you and knew that you were hanging out with the wrong people. You never liked any of them!"

Aden gripped my wrist. He didn't pull my hand away, but his forearm created a very real barrier from us kissing. "If you really love me, then tell me who I love."

I knew in my heart who he loved, but I didn't listen to it. I saw the malice in his eyes and thought it was a sense of betrayal for leaving him. He told me that he didn't love and he all but shouted at me that he didn't even like Fifi, but none of that mattered to me. I gave him the answer that I wanted.

"You love me." It was a foolish thing to say and he didn't even have to tell me I was wrong.

Aden let go of my hand and I brought it back to my chest.

"I love Lily. We could've been together. I knew she felt the same way and we almost were, but she wouldn't. She wouldn't even think of being with me because she knew how much it would hurt you."

I heard what he was saying. I knew what he meant. I was important to them and I let them down. I hurt them to get what I wanted. Lily hurt herself to help her friend get what she wanted.

"She's a really good friend," I told him through my tears.

"Yeah, she is. But you never were. If you were a good friend, you would've told Lily that it was okay for us to date, but that's just not your style, is it, Holly? Lily told me about how she tried to talk to you last year. She told me about how you begged her to stop spending time with me and how you stopped talking to her for a week after I took her out to the movies. Friends don't manipulate each other like that, at least they shouldn't." His words were full of scorn.

Aden didn't care that I was crying. He didn't care that I knew he was right and I wanted nothing more than to make things right. I'd hurt him bad. I kept him and Aily from being happy and what did I get from it? Did Aden magically fall in love with me? Did Aily move on and form a healthy relationship? I wanted Aden because he was my first crush and nothing else mattered to me.

By the time I stopped sobbing, I was alone in the garden.

## 78

**March 20**

I told Aden that he should tell Aily how he feels when he gets back. He didn't say anything. I don't know if he already tried talking to Aily or if the two of them are already dating. I don't think they're dating. They spent a lot of time together when I was crashing at Aily's but that was mostly because they were both mad at me. Maybe their mutual hatred will bring them together. I just wish I could've helped them get there.

I do want them to be happy. I always did, I just wasn't always the best at acting on that. I tried to help Aily find somebody else. I might've stopped talking to Aily for a week, but I was the first to apologize for acting that way. I didn't make her quit Future Authors Club, she did that all her own and came up with some lie about her cousin to protect me. I knew in my heart that she quit because of Aden, but I always thought it was because she asked him out, and he said "no."

Bily kissed Baden, but Aden never mentioned a kiss between them. I wonder if that's why he's still hung up on her. I should ask him, but something tells me I'm not going to get the chance.

Aden and Finn are itching to get out of World B. We literally just got here and they want me to talk to Detective Slauson. I lied about not having his number. I need to find a way to kill Finn. Maybe I can use Detective Slauson to do it somehow. Finn said that he would transform and kill Detective Slauson. That means the plan is to lure Slauson to neutral ground, somewhere that no one can see. How can I use that to set up an ambush against Finn?

Finn knows Brandon by the way. When I mentioned that

my friend Brandon was close to The Gate, Finn got wigged out. He says that we met him, that we both did, but I don't remember. It was during our time as Rainbow Warriors. Brandon was turned into a pupper. We saved him but Finn was the one who went into his mind. When you travel into the mind of a person, you know them almost as well as you know yourself. Brandon was one of the people that stuck with Finn, and he always went back to check on him, but Brandon didn't make it in our world. He was killed by the Troops of Evil.

When I told Finn about Brandon's life, he got sad. He always hoped that without all of the magic that he'd be happy. How can Finn say that good and evil don't exist when there are so many monsters in our world? Rapists, bullies, sexual predators, murderers all live on Earth without the help of Wikella. Does he honestly believe that they're not evil? They deserve to die.

I still don't have a real plan to kill Finn. I could grab a butcher knife from down below, but that would be way too obvious. I need something like a switchblade, and I know Baden has one. But if I go to Baden, he's going to know I'm back. Everyone will know that I'm back and that'll mean that I'm gonna have to make a decision.

I know Aily wants me to go back to their world, but why should I? She only said that because she doesn't understand how much pain I've put her through. Without me, Aily and Aden would already be together, and once I'm out of their life for good, they'll be happier. I know it's what Aily really wants, so why don't I feel happy about it?

Baden loves me, or at the very least, he says he loves me. I don't think he's lying. The way that he kisses me, the way that he holds me is so tender and sweet. Baden might not be my Jad, but he's still a good guy. He's a good guy who got tricked into hooking up with Fifi. He was grieving. Bily was grieving too and she had sex with her violin teacher. Maybe something about losing people makes you horny. I was too young to have those feelings when Olivia died.

But I don't know if I love Baden anymore. It was always Aden that I loved and in a way, I was kind of using Baden. How can I stay behind if it means using him?

Mom's home. Time for an awkward conversation.

# 79

Mom wasn't happy. She was happy to see me back but upset that I left without telling her face to face. She says I don't trust her. Maybe I don't. She wanted to know the truth, I told her that I couldn't tell her the truth, but then Finn did. He just opened his mouth and told her everything. He left out all the specifics of our adventures and didn't talk about my motivations, but he told her that I wasn't her daughter, that the sixteen-year-old girl she buried was never going to come back. Mom was practically catatonic, she stared at the wall the entire time Finn filled her in.

I touched her shoulder and she looked me in the eye and asked, "are you a prostitute?"

I just sighed and told her I was. Mom didn't really talk much after that. I told her we'd be in my room. Finn thinks that my mom will be okay. He wants me to go to the police now, but I can't. I know once we kill Detective Slauson, we're gonna have to leave this world. I'm not ready to say goodbye to World B. Aden said he was gonna find Bily and talk to her. Finn didn't tell me where he was going, but he left the house. They want to attack Slauson tomorrow morning. Aden acted like he'd make me.

I keep thinking about saying goodbye to World B. It was so kind to me, so accepting. The people in this world were nicer to me then mine ever were. Baden and Bily really loved Bolly. She was more open with them and they respected her for it. So why did she kill herself? After all this time, I can't answer that simple question. If I'm really going to say goodbye to this world, I need to read her diary.

## 80

I killed Bolly.

I thought it didn't matter. The Magicals told me that time is endless and infinite. I thought this world would simply exist because it had to. It wasn't like that. Bolly heard us. She heard us talking to her and scrying for another world. She felt a magical pull to think about the Rainbow Warriors and shared my dream of moving to live in the Magical Castle. Every time I went into the mirror to dream of other worlds, the magic reached across the multiverse and filled her head with the same dreams. I wanted her to be just like me without the wand and key but the only way for her to be that close to me, was if she had the exact same experiences.

I reached out through the mirror and imprinted my experiences onto her psyche. While her childhood was fine, high school was a nightmare. The more I stared longingly into the rainbow of time, the more she lost touch with reality. Again and again she talked about "magical dreams" haunting her. She'd be outside trying to live a normal life and then suddenly she'd get visions of me entering the Magical Castle, or share my vision of other worlds.

Her last entry simply said, "I hope this will bring me there."

"This" had to have been suicide, and "there" was undeniably the Magical Castle. She believed they were calling to her. She was consumed with the thought of living in a paradise eternal that she'd seen in half finished dreams and waking hallucinations; visions that my intervention placed into her mind. If I never looked for this world, she would still be alive.

How many lives have I touched by peering through the prism of possibilities? How much of the multiverse have I changed by asking it to find another world?

What have I done?

## 81

**March 21**

I was upset so I went to see Baden. I walked all the way to his house before I texted him. I didn't know if he was even home. I kept thinking about how he was probably with Bily, or Fifi, or maybe he'd moved on to find another girl altogether, but he was home. He came to the door and showed me in. It was almost ten o'clock, but he didn't even ask a single question. He gave me a quick hug and showed me in. His parents weren't downstairs, and I couldn't hear them except for a TV in the master bedroom. Baden had me wait at the top of the stairs. He walked down the hall, the flashing frantic lights of the commercials cast sinister and flattering lights on him one after another.

Baden closed the door to the master bedroom with caution and pity. He was thoughtful and worried. His face was scruffy with stubble, but it was far from a beard. His hair was an unflattering flat mess. When he showed me into his room, I could only really see his white straight teeth against the darkness of the hallway. I entered first. His room was a bit of a sty. I walked in and collected his homework to put it on the floor.

He took his time closing the door, rotating the knob expertly to muffle the noise. He took me into his arms. I could hear him sniffing my hair. I felt every exhale and sigh on my neck. His hands were tender. His arms gripped me with a desperation I matched. He smelled of sweat and worry and I sucked it in. Up close the stink of him was more intoxicating than noxious, like a fly resting on the lip of a pitcher plant. I ran my hands under his shirt and stepped into that trap.

Every attempt he made to speak, I silenced him with a kiss. Slow, half kisses that took his bottom lip into mine. When

I released his lips our eyes met. Trepidation shifted over those gorgeous dark pools. I eased those worries away with a gentle kneading of his flesh, as my fingers trespassed fabric hems, stitched denim, and taboo elastic. He touched me tenderly, afraid to scare me away, but unable to stop himself from feeling the heat of my skin.

I was all fire. Saliva from his kisses melted to steam. His skin was dry tinder and I spread across with the hunger of a flame, one that was never satiated. I met the wind of his breath with licking tendrils full of need. I seared my name onto his lips and scarred his flesh with the shape of me. I consumed him fully and he crackled and broke to my inferno.

My conflagration burned away his hesitation and worries. He was made to bear my passion and it became us. We were united in our lust and all attempts to utter a word the other smothered with their lips. No requests were given but no needs were left unsatiated. He put everything he was into our coupling and I scratched our commitment onto his back. Denied of the ability to express our love with words we forced it out of our bodies.

He was sweaty and magnificent after the fact. I'd never seen a more beautiful man, nor a more honest expression. I told him, "say it."

He eagerly replied, "I love you."

When I asked him to say it again, he did so with a kiss. I asked this task of him again and again until somehow we'd switched roles and I confessed my undying love for a man that I couldn't truly name. All I knew was that he was Jad. He was what my heart longed for and I couldn't deny it anymore. I loved him with everything I was and we fell asleep comparing each other to perfect sunsets and undying cosmos.

Did I use him? I don't know. In the moment, all I could think about was him and how I wanted our coupling with all of my soul. I went to him hoping to talk, but once I was there, all I could think about was how much I wanted him. He'll call me tomorrow, or this morning I should say. I'm going to have to explain that I'm leaving and that last night was goodbye, but I don't regret it. I don't regret what we shared. Since that first day we made out, I wanted him to take me as his lover. Now that he has, I want it to happen all over again.

How can I leave someone that loves me like that?

Do I really care about sex more than my friends and family?

Will I still feel this way when I wake?

If I do, maybe I'm just a bad person; maybe I always have been.

# 82

I just got through talking to Baden on the phone. He wants to come over, but I repeatedly told him not to. There's too much weird magic stuff going on. I can't have him getting mixed up in it. It was hard enough to say goodbye over the phone. I did it. I told him that I was living on borrowed time, that my return came with a cost and that it was a cost that I couldn't pay. He kept asking me to elaborate, but I didn't. All I could do was try to convince him that I love him and that I was sorry.

Things have gotten so complicated in my mind. It's like a house with a new door everywhere I turn. Every closet door leads to a hallway or a living room and those doors lead to bedrooms which in turn have closets. I need to clean this house. I need to pick up all my things and vacuum the floor, but there's no end to the mess in one room. Every bit of rubbage is part of a thick pile without end and I have nowhere to put everything even if I did.

I close my eyes and five different problems come rushing in at once. Should I stay here? How do I tell Bily goodbye? How can I stop Slauson and Finn? How am I going to kill Wikella? How do I make up for all the wrong that I've done? Maybe I can't undo everything. I feel like going back to live in my own world is a start.

Aily was right. People don't have an escape. People have to live with the lives that they have. If they want things to be better they have to work to get those better lives, even if they're not perfect. Is growing up just about getting better at making compromises? I really hope this is just a high school thing, but what kind of job am I even going to have? I have no skills. My grades are shishido peppers seeds: small and edible.

Finn is here. I'm going to text everyone goodbye, and then I'm calling Detective Slauson. I can't keep stalling.

## 83

Tiff said that she was really going to miss me. She told me to find another way to stay. She said that even if it meant becoming a fallen angel, that I should fall from grace. According to her heaven is overrated. It probably is, most lies are.

Talking to Brandon was different. He didn't try to bargain. Brandon just wanted to thank me. He knew that my kiss didn't mean anything to me, but it meant a lot to him. He kept looking in the mirror and touching his malformed lips and saying, "she kissed me." Knowing he was kissable felt good. He told me that he has a crush on me and that he's liked me since the first moment he saw me, but he thought that something couldn't ever happen between us. Even though he was right, he was wrong.

I would've kissed Brandon back. I would've been his girlfriend. He has a beautiful heart and a celestial mind. Every time I talk to him I reconsider my life and see my past with fresh eyes. He's the kind of person I need in my life, even if it's just as a friend. It doesn't help me to surround myself with people who think like I do or even like each other. Moving forward, I need to be friends with people that aren't popular. I don't think he even wants to be popular.

Brandon's going to try going back to school. He said that he couldn't have done that without me. I don't think that's true. I think Brandon is going back to school because he's a brave person who really understands his soul, but maybe I helped him in a small way. Either way, I'm glad he's gonna try again. I hope it works out.

Thinking about Brandon and Tiff gives me hope. I didn't trick them into liking me. They became my friends because of who I am and there will be people like them in my world. I'll be able to start over with new friends and this time I'm not going to hurt them. This time I'm going to tell them everything. No matter what happens with my attempt on Finn's life, I'm not going back to the Magical Castle. I'm going to break the Oath and try to live a normal life.

Calling Bily was hard.

I didn't think she would even answer the phone. She answered with a cold, "what?"

"I'm leaving soon. I wanted to apologize and say goodbye. Please don't hang up." When she didn't answer I did my best to make things right and be honest. I don't have a lot of experience with that second one.

"It's okay that you're mad at me. I hurt a lot of people to be here, so I'm not coming back. I just wanted you to know that I'm sorry. I'm sorry for coming here and playing with your emotions. Your Holly loved you, she loved you more than I ever could. I want you to know that her leaving had nothing to do with you. Every month, every week that she was alive was in part because of you. You helped her so much! You made it easier for her to deal with life and kept things from being hopeless, but she couldn't keep it up.

"You once described the pain of isolation as being a white rabbit in summer. For her, it was like being a caged rabbit on the windowsill. She could see the warren. She remembered what the grass and her friends smelled like, but it wasn't something she experienced anymore. All she could do was stare out that window and wish for a better life. She would've wanted to apologize to you too. She couldn't keep waiting for that cage to open."

Bily was crying on the other line. I waited a moment for her to say something, when she didn't I said goodbye.

"Holly."

"Yeah."

"Don't...don't give up on that cage. Okay?"

"Okay. I love you."

She sniffed back tears and told me, "good luck."

Finn is back. Everything is going to happen now. Three

people lie between me and a normal life. I can kill three more. I can still save the world.

# 84

I had Detective Slauson meet us at the gate. I made Brandon promise me that no matter what he heard outside, that he wouldn't come to help. Detective Slauson was walking into a trap and no one was going to save him, least of all the police. Finn was focused. He looked ready to kill. Aden didn't say much of anything. He was posted up on a low hanging branch.

"Hands up!" Was the detective's way of saying hello.

He came out from behind a tree with a gun trained on me. I thought Finn would transform but he just did as he was asked. Was it some kind of illusion? Could Finn make illusions without needing to transform? I don't know. He never explained how he could teleport from Ohio to The Gate. Maybe he wasn't worried about the gun aimed at my chest because he could stop the bullet.

"This isn't necessary, Detective. We're all willing to cooperate," Finn told him.

Detective Slauson looked us over and changed his target to Finn. "Who are you?"

"My name is Finn, Detective Slauson. I'm going to tell you all about the magic wand in your pocket and we're going to use that magic key together. Did you come alone?"

"Not a chance. The place is surrounded. You kids try anything they'll be on you like white on rice," he growled.

"You don't need to lie to me, Detective Slauson. I know all about the ongoing investigation."

"How do you know about that?" He looked twitchy.

I tried to back away to the trees and the shaved gorilla swung the piece my way. I might've pissed my panties.

"On me, Detective Slauson. Holly isn't going to hurt you. None of us are. I know about the investigation for the same reason I know about your divorce and the tragic end of your son's life. I'm magic, Detective Slauson, all three of us are. We're travelers from another world. I don't know if your son is alive in our world, but we can help you find a world where he is."

The big man lowered his gun. "What's in it for you?"

"I get to help a man who got dealt a bad hand."

I was convinced it was a trick, but Finn sounded calm and collected. When the detective finally put his gun away, Finn offered him his hand. They shook.

"I'm Finn."

"Detective Slauson. Sorry about the gun."

"It's not a problem. All of that is behind you now. You don't need to worry about Internal Affairs or your mother's mortgage. You're safe. You get to live the life that you want. Whatever life you want, we'll find a way to get you there. Can I have the wand?"

Slauson handed it over.

"That's mine, Finn. Don't double cross me."

Finn didn't even look at me. He kept his eyes on the big man. "Are you ready to go through The Gate?"

He nodded. The big guy wiped tears out of his eyes. "It's really going to happen? Magic is real."

"You're a solid detective, Slauson. You didn't miss a thing. Terrance would've been proud."

Now the lummox really was crying.

Finn was in complete control and there was nothing I could do to stop him. I should've known he'd use the wand to enter Slauson's dreams and get him on his side. Finn's word was useless. He didn't believe in good or evil or oaths or promises. He was a selfish boy, willing to destroy the Magicals just to have sex with a cartoon witch.

"Jaden, are you ready?"

My bearded former crush nodded.

"I want you to go in first. Do you still remember how to open The Gate?"

"I'll never forget it."

"Slauson, would you give Jaden the key?"

Slauson frowned, but did as he was bid. He could've

snapped Aden's neck. Instead, he took out the tiny green key and handed it over. Aden walked up to the curved trees at the edge of the woods. Their trunks and branches arched inwards to form the sides of a perfect circle. No moss grew on the insides, no insects wandered their bark. They were apart from our world, existing in the material plane like a cloud in the ocean.

Aden held the key over his head and slowly formed a circle as he spoke the password, "open sesame."

Slauson guffawed. He couldn't help it. He laughed so hard that he leaned against Aden for support. The man looked like he might bust a gut, save his fixation on the ripple between worlds.

At first glance, the edge between our worlds looked like a shimmer on the surface of a rippling pond. Between the crests and swells of the translucent film, glimpses of the Magical Castle came in like reflections. Technicolor battlements and banners rolled on the air slower than the rainbow film on the surface of an oil spill. Aden stepped through and the film popped, showing cartoon guardians wielding halberds the size of light posts.

Slauson stepped to the edge of The Gate and gazed forward with awe. On the other side, Aden waved him in. He put his hand through and chuckled. "It tickles. It's like getting licked by a puppy."

Finn smiled back at him. "Like the fuzziest kind with the wettest nose."

Laughing, the man began to cry as magic finally entered his life. He stepped through, ran up to Aden and hugged him. The grown man picked up Aden in his embrace and laughed as he spun them around. Even though I couldn't hear his laughter, I could see it on his face.

"Is this where you double cross me, Finn?" After everything I'd been through, I was ready to die. I just didn't want him to have the satisfaction of thinking that he'd somehow outsmarted me.

Finn chuckled. "No, Holly. I told you before, I'm here as a favor to you. I'm here because I used to call you Greenie, the Mean M&M, and you called me Rude Boy. We were friends,

Holly, and I never apologized for turning my back on you. I didn't think you would understand. I hope you will one day. Wikella was never a bad person. Being evil was the only way for her to survive. I don't think anyone is really evil given those circumstances."

I knew he was wrong, but there was no point in telling him that. Once we were through the gate, I'd find a way to jam Baden's flip blade into his side. I'd already practiced flipping it out without looking at it. Maybe I could even steal Slauson's gun. It shouldn't be too hard to get the bear to the baths now that the grizzly was a teddy. Finn was going to die by my hand.

He stepped out of my way and I walked up to The Gate and hit a wall.

"Oof. What?" I slapped my hand against the translucent film between our worlds and it felt harder than steel. There was no give. The ripples of the waves weren't caused by my hand, they were remnants of Slauson's entrance. A man that was investigated by Internal Affairs could walk through the gate of morality, but I, who had suffered so much, couldn't return to the world I was born to.

"I thought as much," Finn said with a little sigh. He pulled out his red key and held it out to me.

I shook my head. "I'm not a bad person, Finn. I'm not! I never broke the Oath. I haven't said a curse word in almost ten years!"

"I told you that none of that mattered. You feel guilty. You don't believe you're a good person and that's all The Gate can sense. I didn't enter your mind and I don't want to. If you can forgive yourself and return, you're welcome to, but I'm not going to stay here and get tangled up in this. Take the key, Holly, and say goodbye."

I could still kill him. I could loose the blade and slash his wrist. Even though I wasn't a good person, I'd still have the seven wands. I could find seven kids and train them how to fight evil and prepare them for the battle against Wikella. Killing Finn would make sure that Wikella's plot wouldn't work.

But I didn't take that path.

Finn was my friend. Maybe he hadn't been in a long time, but at one point he was. We would tease each other and laugh at all of our terrible jokes. We went to water parks together and pet the same giraffe. We held each other when we cried and pushed each other while we yelled everything but a swear word. He was my friend and as strange as it was, he was happy with Wikella, and I didn't want to take that from him.

"Fucking shit, Finn." I started crying.

He hugged me and I cried into his shoulder while he rubbed my back.

"I'm sorry, Holly. I wish I could take you with me."

"I was good!" I sobbed. "I was so fucking good!"

"I know, Holly. You did your best. That's all any of us ever can." He hugged me tight and pulled back to look me in the eyes. I could barely see him through my tears or hear him through my whimpering. "Whatever you've done. Whatever cruelties you've brought on the world, you did it because you thought it was best. I hope that one day you'll realize that and forgive yourself."

I could only nod and hug him again, tighter than before. I hugged him until my arms were tired. "Finn, can you tell me what happened to Sashy? Is she happy?"

"She is. You and her are in a pop band. You call yourself Sour Bubblegum. Her boyfriend is the lead guitarist and your girlfriend never misses a show."

"Girlfriend?" I chuckled.

Finn shrugged. "Infinite timelines, right? I guess that's something that you can figure out for yourself. If you ever come back to our world, look for me and Wikella."

"You're not going to rule over the Magical Castle?"

Finn shook his head. "I never wanted that and neither did Wikella, not really. All she ever wanted was to live in peace and she has that now. We're gonna grow old together and raise a family...if she can get pregnant."

I smiled at that. "I think you'll be a good dad."

"Thank you, Holly." He kissed my forehead. "I love you,

Greenie."

"I love you too, Rude Boy."

We shared one last hug and then I had to let him go. I said goodbye to him and the mystic gate to a cartoon world where I could be anyone or do anything. I said goodbye to my magic wand that let me transform into judge, jury, and executioner. I said goodbye to saving the world. Maybe one day I'll say goodbye to good and evil.

# EPILOGUE

**December 26**

Dear Diary,

Today's the one year anniversary of Bolly's death. There's been some talk about unearthing her corpse and seeing if the skeleton is still in there, but Mom's told them to fuck off. She left Dad. We live in this small house, but I'm closer to school and my neighbors are really nice. I still see Dad when I can. As far as divorces go, it seems like a good one. They haven't argued about custody and I can go visit him whenever I want. He's in AA now and he's told me that he's accepted Jesus into his heart. He tells me that he prays for me. I know he does, but I still don't think he believes it.

Mom still hasn't started dating, but she's been checking out this gardener. I've been doing my best to nudge her in his direction. She's scared to start something new, but I told her that she can just fuck and not call him. It makes her laugh. I like seeing Mom smile. I really missed that.

Oh, they actually made that Lifetime story about me. They got this really cute girl to play me. She's 19 and her only acting experience before this was shaking her butt in a music video. It's about as bad as I thought it would be. They really played up my relationship with Jaden and they made Fifi out to be this generic latina bitch. She even had a blonde wig and dressed like Legally Blonde's niece. The whole movie is pure cringe from start to finish, but I loved watching it with Tiff and the volleyball girls.

I'm still friends with Tiff. She's kind of my bestie now. She still can't find a boyfriend to save her life and she's been joking about "trying girls," a lot. I've tried to be supportive without being pushy. I don't think she's anything but straight personally, but any girl would be lucky to have her.

Ummm, Jaden and I aren't together anymore. I guess he's supposed to be Baden because I'm in World B. I don't think about the World B-World A thing anymore. He's just Jaden in my mind.

The first week or so after I said goodbye to Finn, I was a wreck. I was crying a lot and I said "I'm sorry," for every little thing. I still do that. I kind of get teased for it, but it ain't a thing. Anyway, during that time I was kind of trying to push Jaden and Lily together and that drove a rift into my relationship with both of them. Lily got sick of me trying to steer her life and I was never able to open up to Jaden. Every little fight we had, I got it into my head that he'd be happier with Lily.

When Jaden finally came up to end things, I saw it in his eyes and ended it first. He thanked me for making it easier on him and I apologized for pushing him away. The last thing he told me as my boyfriend was to make me promise that I wouldn't apologize so much. True to form, I told him, "sorry," and we laughed about it.

Lily is doing okay now, but it was really touch and go for a while. Pretty much everyone but Amber isn't her friend now. According to some, I stole her friends from her, but I'm a lot closer to Tiff and her friends than Lily's old circle of friends. I think they fell out because Lily was just tired of being that person.

It got easier to talk to Lily after Jaden and I were done. About three months after the breakup she called me and I finally talked to her without apologizing for ruining their life. She still misses Bolly a lot, but she considers me a good friend. Lily dropped violin by the way, she keeps going back and forth from being an artist or a writer. I think she's going to be one of those respected cartoonists who draws thoughtful biographies. She really understands what people are going through and it shows in her writing.

I never rejoined Future Authors Club, but I am a member of the school's Gay Straight Alliance. I haven't started kissing girls and I still haven't wanted to. I identify as straight and no one in the club gives me any problems about it. Most of the time we just eat pizza and talk about all the bigotry in the world. Sometimes I get really heated about all of the injustices and I have to remind myself that I'm not a Rainbow Warrior. Any change that happens has to be part of a larger movement. I've written some Senators and Governors, but I've been staying off social media. I feel like if I jump into that with my notoriety as Lazarus Girl, it's only going to be a matter of time before I say something everyone doesn't like. Tiff thinks I'm being a chicken, but she doesn't know what I'm trying to overcome.

I still haven't told Tiff about my past as a Rainbow Warrior, and I like it better that way. Talking to Lily and Mom has helped with a lot of that. When I have my panic attacks and get bad flashbacks I call Lily or wake Mom up and we talk it out. Mom says that helping me has helped her and that makes me feel better about bugging her everyday.

I tried The Gate again today. It was the first time in at least six months that I have. Last time I was with Mom and she had this look on her face like, "well, it's probably better that I'm here." The Gate didn't work for me, of course. I still hate myself. I think a lot about how I hurt the people in World A and how I hurt the people in World B and how I continue to hurt people in World B. I know that I need to forgive myself, but I can't even say the words.

I ran into Brandon. He saw me at The Gate and asked if we could sit and talk. He's doing great! Before he was a metalhead, but he was kind of like this shy metalhead that hid his weird. Now he's wearing his weird on his sleeves and it suits him! He's got these cool plug extenders that look like black spikes in his ears and he wears black eyeshadow. But that's not even the best part! Not only did he go back to school, but he has a girlfriend! When I saw his picture with her at a Pantera cover band, I lost my shit! He and Fifi are a thing and they look so happy together!

I was so lost in my conversation with Brandon that I almost didn't see the lunch box on the ground. It's a Sailor Jupiter lunch box and I might use it to bring my lunches to school. Inside was a letter from Finn.

He used the seven wands to make Wikella a sixteen-year-old human girl. They're still together and they've been all over the world. True to form, Finn used his magic to get independently wealthy and they're living in New York in a high rise overlooking Central Park, which I guess is a big deal. They have tutors come over to teach the two of them about math, science, history, and all of the things they'll need to get into a good ivy league college. Wikella was thinking about becoming a lawyer, but Finn says he wants to keep experimenting with the wands. He says that he's close to doing something big, but he doesn't want to jinx it by talking about it.

Finn visited the Magicals, of course. He says they tried to kill him and he had to blow up a few towers before they calmed down. He offered all of them the chance to change into humans and a bunch of them are going to do it. Among them are Princess Platypus and King Walrus, but not the queen. I guess my parents aren't the only ones getting a divorce.

He visited Sashy before he talked to me and he included a USB with Sour Bubblegum's music. I play the drums and I sound really good. It feels so good to hear Sashy's voice! I hope she's doing well. Finn says she's in a rough spot right now, but he's confident that she'll get through it. That other-other Holly is still with the same girl! She must be something special.

Lily and Jaden from World A didn't want to write me. Finn said that mentioning my name still hurts them and I can't blame them for that. Hell, I'm the same way. I hate hearing my name. He did include their picture though and he says they're engaged to be engaged. I'm really glad they found happiness. They're going to be great parents, I just know it!

As for me, I'm trying.

I don't think about growing old surrounded by cartoons anymore and I haven't actively thought about suicide in three months. I know that's not ideal, but that's progress for me and my therapist says it's good to celebrate every victory. We still haven't found a good medication, but we're working on finding the right cocktail to deal with my comorbidity. I've been telling her about the Rainbow Warriors here and there but Dr. Vargas doesn't really know how to deal with it. Basically, I'm learning techniques to cope and trying to process my past when I can. At this rate I should be guilt free by 2167.

I'm okay with that. I'm okay with never going back to World A or seeing Lily and Jad again. I left that world. I hurt everyone there and they don't owe me anything. My reappearance would just hurt my bio mom and dad, so it's probably better if I just stay where I am.

I'm writing this, Diary, because it's time to say goodbye. This paper and these pens are from World A. Though unlikely, they continue to threaten a paradox and so they need to be destroyed. I know that you were part of a spell to help children cope with their trauma, but you were a good friend. You helped me through some of the worst times in my life and without you, I think I would've given up on life a long time ago. So, thank you, Diary, for everything.

I still have no clue what I'm going to do after graduation, but I haven't given up on life. I feel excited by the possibilities! I'm in theater working behind the scenes and I'm gonna try jumping into acting. I'm the worst defender in the soccer team, but every day at practice I feel a little better. No matter what happens, there's a different Holly that I can be.

I just have to keep living.